4.46

Newma

D0829035

TROUBLE AT THE TOP OF THE WORLD

Roy MacGregor

McClelland & Stewart

JPB MacGr
582
Apr. 3/09
Copy 1

For Fisher David Cation, first grandchild, future Owl.

COPYRIGHT © 2008 BY ROY MACGREGOR

All rights reserved. The use of any part of this publication reproduced,
transmitted in any form or by any means, electronic, mechanical,
photocopying, recording, or otherwise, or stored in a retrieval
system, without the prior written consent of the publisher –
or, in case of photocopying or other reprographic copying, a
licence from the Canadian Copyright Licensing Agency – is an
infringement of the copyright law.

Library and Archives Canada Cataloguing in Publication

MacGregor, Roy, 1948–
    Trouble at the top of the world / Roy MacGregor.
(The Screech Owls series; #22)
ISBN 978-0-7710-5609-3

    I. Title. II. Series: MacGregor, Roy, d1948– .
Screech Owls series.

PS8575.G84T46 2009   jC813'.54   C2008-904243-3

We acknowledge the financial support of the Government of Canada
through the Book Publishing Industry Development Program and
that of the Government of Ontario through the Ontario Media
Development Corporation's Ontario Book Initiative. We further
acknowledge the support of the Canada Council for the Arts and the
Ontario Arts Council for our publishing program.

Typeset in Bembo by M&S, Toronto
Printed and bound in Canada

McClelland & Stewart Ltd.
75 Sherbourne Street
Toronto, Ontario
M5A 2P9
www.mcclelland.com

1 2 3 4 5   13 12 11 10 09

Newmarket Public Library

Wayne Nishikawa

YO!

This is the Ol' Nisherama – World's Number-One-Ranked Peewee Hockey Player, future star of the National Hockey League, Funniest Human Being on Earth, in the Galaxy, in the Universe, holder of the Guinness World Record for the number of people mooned in a single flick of the old belt buckle.

How do ya do?

I am sitting here completely in the dark.

It's hot in here, but at least I don't have to listen to Travis natter on about all-day sunlight and icebergs, and Sarah and Sam squealing about stupid polar bears.

The only drawback to this is that all I can smell is brown paper bag. I feel like somebody's stale lunch.

I THINK I'M GONNA HURL!!!!!!!!!!!!

1

Don Dillinger

I'D BETTER EXPLAIN.

I'd like to tell you where I'm writing this from, but I haven't a clue, to tell the truth. Somewhere in the sky over the very top of the world, I guess. All I know is that if you went straight down, you'd hit ice. And if you kept on going straight down, you'd hit more ice.

We are somewhere over the Arctic Circle. We're headed for the Inuit village of Pangnirtung – or, as they call it, "Pang" – in the territory of Nunavut. And, frankly, I'm a bit nervous. If I look out of this old twin-prop plane, I can only see clouds. Somehow, the pilot's going to have to punch through that thick cover and land on a gravel strip in the middle of nowhere and bring this shuddering, shaking old plane to a halt before it slams into the side of a hill.

I can't let the kids see I'm scared, though. Especially Nish, who is sitting just across the aisle with a brown paper bag over his head. Travis, who is Nish's best friend, claims he does this so he won't hyperventilate, but I say he does it because he doesn't want to see anything. He's terrified of heights, you know. And afraid of flying.

I wouldn't be surprised if he tossed his cookies – wouldn't be the first time, that's for sure.

At least if he has to "hurl" – as he loves to shout out in the most embarrassing places possible – the barf bag's already there!

Okay, I've got to explain. Sorry about that.

I'm writing this for an "assignment." Crazy, I know, especially for a grown man with so little hair he hasn't had to comb it for years, but true all the same. A Grade Eight assignment, no less – and me a college graduate!

But I've got to do it; it was the only way I could get all the Screech Owls to buy in. If *we* have to do this, Sarah said to me in front of the whole team, then *you'll* have to do it, too.

I couldn't escape.

But that was the deal we struck with the school. The Owls all get to miss classes for a week to take this amazing trip into the Far North and play in a hockey tournament, but in return they all have to keep a journal. The principal insisted. So it's a hockey trip, but it's also a school excursion. Every single person on the team contributes to a journal, Fahd and Data take the photographs and video, and at the end we put it together as an educational presentation on Canada's newest territory for all the kids at Lord Stanley Public School. Once it's completed, the school plans to put it up on a Web site so all the other schools in the country can check it out.

Fair enough. As team manager, I was the one who had to go to the principal to ask permission, and the only way she would give it was if we turned the experience into something educational as well as a hockey tournament.

The only kid who's complained about keeping a journal so far is, of course, Nishikawa. No surprise there.

The girls, on the other hand, were terrific. Sarah and Sam are going to do their own separate project on polar bears – presuming we see one or two while we're here.

How we got here is a story in itself. A few months back, I received a letter with "Rideau Hall" embossed on the envelope. I have to admit, my first thought was that I had been awarded the Order of Canada for my volunteer work with the team and the hospital, but it had nothing to do with me at all.

Dear Mr. Dillinger,
This coming June 21st, the Governor General of Canada will be travelling to Pangnirtung, an Inuit village on Baffin Island in the territory of Nunavut, to take part in the 24/7 Sunlight

Festival. As part of the celebrations, the Inuit organizers will be staging a small peewee hockey tournament involving teams from Pangnirtung, Resolute, and Iqaluit.

The organizers have requested that a fourth team be invited from Southern Canada, and your recent performance at the Bell Capital Cup in Ottawa suggests that your team would be ideal for this adventure.

If the Screech Owls of Tamarack are able to go, the Government of Canada would be pleased to bring the team, its coach, and its manager to Pangnirtung for the festival. All accommodation and food would be looked after by the organizers. The Governor General sees this as an excellent opportunity for young boys and girls from other parts of Canada to see what Canadian youngsters are like in the Far North and, if you are interested, we ask only that you arrange with the school involved so that time could be given over to what will be a highly educational trip as well as a first-rate hockey tournament.

The Governor General looks forward to your early reply.

Well, what would *you* say?
Of course I said "YES!"

Travis Lindsay

THIS IS MY FIRST "JOURNAL" ENTRY. I THINK it's an excellent idea – it will mean we'll have a great record of everything that happens on this trip.

We're playing in a tournament against teams we've never even heard of, let alone seen, so we have no idea how they play. But then, we're not sure how *we'll* play, either – the Owls haven't been on the ice since our last tournament two months ago.

Muck hates summer hockey and tells us never to sign up for it. "Play another sport," our coach says, "soccer or lacrosse or baseball or golf – any skill you pick up there will help every other sport you play. You'll all be better hockey players in the fall if you do something entirely different in the summer."

But Muck agreed to this, much to our surprise. A chance of a lifetime, he called it. A learning experience. Which is why all of us, with one exception, sort of like the idea of the journals.

We had only one player who couldn't make it – Liz Moscovitz had her appendix out last week. So Jesse Highboy put a call in to his cousin, Rachel, and she flew from James Bay to Iqaluit, the capital of Nunavut, and joined us when we changed from the jet to this old propeller plane. Now Nish is sitting there with that stupid paper bag over his head – scared out of his wits. He says he hyperventilates when he gets to high altitudes. I say he freaks out, simple as that.

I couldn't be happier. Rach and I have been writing back and forth ever since that great trip to Waskaganish where Nish put the snowmobile through the ice and Jesse and Rachel's grandfather played goal with a shovel for a stick.

There's so much excitement about this trip. The sun will be shining all day long – no "night" at all. And we'll be able to go out on the ice, and we may even see a polar bear.

Mr. D. says there is a big "feast" planned for Tuesday evening at the community centre. We all had to bring hunting knives so we could "serve" ourselves.

"Everybody here like sushi?" Mr. D. asked at the team meeting we had last week.

"We *invented* sushi!" Nish boasted.

"Well, you better like it," said Mr. D. "That feast will include seal and fish and caribou, and maybe, just maybe, even walrus. None of it cooked. Everything just as if your mother had carried it home that day from the butcher. You'll have to use your own knives to cut off a piece and eat it raw. I'm not kidding."

"I'M GONNA HURL!!!"

Sarah Cuthbertson

YOU HAD TO SEE IT TO BELIEVE IT.

Three o'clock in the morning, and Travis was driving off the first – and *only* – tee of the World's Craziest Golf Course.

It was a good thing the sun was shining – brighter at 3:00 A.M. than it had been at midnight – because the ball instantly headed for trouble.

Travis's drive flew high and hard off the flat rock that served as the driving tee. It slammed into the face of the cliff that rose up toward the village. It bounced, hit another rock, bounced, hit a third rock, bounced back, hit a fourth rock, and went straight over the cliff and down onto the frozen Arctic Ocean and its jumble of green-blue ice.

"You're dead meat!" chuckled Nish, already teeing up his ball.

"Maybe not," I corrected him. "If he can find it, he can play it – that's the rule."

"They said it's better to stay off the ice," Travis said. "The bay usually stays frozen until September – but there are already gaps of open water. If it's sunk, I'll hit another."

Nish was paying no attention. He was whipping his golf club back and forth, trying to stand like Tiger Woods and look like he knew exactly what he was doing, instead of like Wayne Nishikawa, who doesn't have a clue what he's doing.

"I'm shooting for the fairway," he announced.

"Fat chance, Fat Boy," I told him. I'd already hit, and we could see my ball, playable if not exactly on the fairway.

Fairway is an interesting word here. It stands out because it's green – but the colour has nothing to do with grass.

The Pang Golf & Country Club has

- no grass
- no trees
- no sand
- no water, except for frozen
- only one hole, approximately six hundred metres long
- no penalties for lost balls
- no charge
- a scrap of green outdoor carpet to tee off on, a slightly larger piece of carpet called the "fairway," and a small, round piece of

carpet with a hole in the middle to serve as the "green"
- a broken fishing pole with a bandana tied to it for a "pin"

And yet, I'd have to say that Travis and I, both having gone out a couple of times with Travis's grandfather to the fancy-dancy Tamarack Golf & Country Club, have never enjoyed a game of golf so much.

For sure, we've never laughed so hard playing the game. Laughing makes it different. At the Tamarack course, people speak in whispers, and not at all when they are anywhere close to a green. You'd think you were in a library, not at a sports event.

At the Pang course, players yell and scream all they like. Even fall down laughing, just as Trav and I did when Nish's second drive took off straight into a rock and flew right back into Nish's roly-poly gut, knocking him to the ground as if he'd been hit by lightning.

"I'M DEAD!!!!!!!!!"

There we were, all three of us lying on the ground – two of us laughing so hard we had tears in our eyes, one of us crying so hard he had tears in his eyes.

"You're *not* dead!" Travis told Nish once he stopped the stupid wailing. "You're still up! Your shot again!"

Travis and I started to get to our feet, still laughing, when suddenly we hit the ground again, hard.

There was this unbelievable *roar* overhead.

We looked up, straight into the open side of a huge helicopter that seemed close enough to reach up and clip with one of our clubs.

"*What the – !*"Travis shouted.

I could barely hear him over the roar of the engines, and then the wind from the rotor hit us, almost ripping the skin from our cheeks.

We all turned our faces into the ground while the wind pinned us to the spot as if roofing nails were being driven into our windbreakers.

Then, in another instant, it was gone, the roar moving off down the coastline.

"What was *that?*" Nish shouted as he turned right side up and began getting to his feet.

"Helicopter," Travis said. "I could see its side panel open before the wind hit us – two guys were inside taking video of everything."

Nish let the air pop out of his big cheeks. "I didn't think my swing was *that* good!"

"I don't think they were interested in golfers," I said. "I saw them too. Looked mean."

"Probably just bored," said Travis. "Government workers, doing maps or something."

I let it go, but didn't seem like that to me.

Nish was already teeing up again. He swung, and this time the ball took off over the sheer rock face, clipped off a rock, ticked another, skipped on a third, and popped straight onto the tiny little "fairway" that had seemed impossible to hit.

Nish turned, bowed in several directions to an invisible cheering crowd, then delivered one of his famous wet raspberries.

"You're there in three," I pointed out. "Rules of the game."

"How do you have *rules* in an insane game like this?" Nish muttered, slamming his club into his bag and heading off along the rock path toward his ball.

"I'm there in one," he shouted back, his face beet red. "First shot didn't count – Travis was talking."

I looked at Travis, who just rolled his eyes. Even when it doesn't matter, Nish can't stand to lose.

I guess I have to admit, though, that he's the same when it does matter. And for the Screech Owls, that's a *good* thing.

Dmitri Yakushev

I DIDN'T LIKE THIS "JOURNAL" THING WHEN I first heard about the deal. I have enough trouble talking to people about what I'm doing – let alone writing it all down for everyone to read.

Besides, I didn't think I'd have anything to write about.

Ha! Where to begin?

Last night – though it seems crazy to use the word *night* around here – they held a feast at the community centre to welcome the Governor General. The whole village came out for the official arrival, and the streets of Pang filled with people kicking up dust as they walked to the gravel airstrip.

When the Governor General's plane landed, the dust was like a cloud settling over the village. But it cleared soon enough, and the doors eventually opened and all the big shots came out and stood at attention while a little band played "O Canada" and we all tried to sing along. The Governor General then inspected an honour guard of "Rangers" – mostly a rag-tag bunch of old men in red sweatshirts carrying rifles that looked like they were left over from World War One. There were even a couple of teenagers and one or two women. Nish was making fun of them until Muck reached over and gave him the quickest little cuff to the back of the head you ever saw – almost like a towel snap – and told him to show a little respect. Muck said these were the same as soldiers or policemen where we came from.

Nish turned so red he looked a bit like a Ranger himself.

When the Owls arrived at the community centre, the food had already been spread out on three different plastic sheets – tarps, someone called them – that were placed directly on the floor. No tables, no chairs – and no cutlery. Mr. D. had told us all to make sure and bring our own hunting knives, and we soon found out why.

The blue tarp held slabs of red, bloody caribou. You could still see some fur on parts and one hoof. A green tarp had a bunch of thick slabs of some other kind of meat on it, all bloody and red. Sarah said they were seals. She didn't look too happy. I went over and looked, and you could see the seals' eyes and faces – everything was there, it seemed, but their skin. A yellow tarp had all sorts of different fish

15

on it. They said there was Arctic char, sea trout, and salmon. They were lying there whole as if they'd just been hauled into a boat. Nish claimed he saw one still flipping around! I don't know about that, but they couldn't have been dead long. None of the "meal" – seals, fish, caribou – could have been long dead. Everything was bloody and glistening, and while half the Owls were walking around like they were about to throw up, the excitement among the Inuit was wild. It was like they'd come to a fall fair. Or a Stanley Cup playoff.

The old people ate first. They called them elders, and some were wearing fur outfits that looked like a few hours ago they might have been on some of the food that was being served. And people were wearing sealskin boots. One older man even had on thick, snow-white boots – Sam said they were polar bear fur. Her lower lip was trembling when she told me this.

It was like nothing any of us had ever imagined. The old folks tore into the food like they hadn't eaten for weeks and had just walked into a deli. And some of them didn't seem to even have teeth! They were laughing and giggling and using their big knives to saw off chunks of meat and pieces of fish, and they were practically fighting over one seal after one of the men gutted it with his knife and spilled out its black insides.

"*EVERYBODY'S* GONNA HURL!" screamed Nish.

But no one did. The elders ate, and then, one by one, they came over and invited the Governor General and the officials to join in the feast. Then, once they had that group settled, each of them took an Owl over to taste some of the delicacies. I used my knife to cut off some pieces to try. I've even had food like this before, when I travelled into northern Siberia with my Uncle Aleksei. They have Inuit there, too, only they don't call them that. They called themselves Yupik.

Mr. D. says, when he was a boy, people who lived around the North Pole were all called Eskimos, but that name isn't used any longer in Canada. They're Inuit and they speak Inuktitut – but a lot of them also speak English, so we were fine.

I liked the food. Nish went around bragging that he was Japanese and the Japanese invented eating raw fish, but I didn't see him each much of anything. In fact, he looked about as white as I've ever seen my chubby buddy look.

Sarah and Sam had big trouble eating anything. Sam was in tears until one of the elders who spoke English took her aside for a long talk, and when Sam came back she seemed okay about things. But by then the meat and fish were being rolled up in the tarps and taken away anyway. Then they brought out a typical North American meal – complete with hot dogs, hamburgers, and pizza-flavoured potato chips.

Nish suddenly had his colour *and* his appetite back.

We ate at tables this time, and they sat us with people from the village, who seemed shy but at the same time very friendly. A couple of kids said they were on the local hockey team, but we didn't talk much hockey, except to argue about who will win next year's Stanley Cup.

After the feast, they had a party. We sat and watched dancers and musicians and drummers, and several women came out in couples and did something called throat singing, which is just about the craziest, weirdest sound you ever imagined. Most of them looked like mothers and daughters, or sisters, and they'd get really close to each other and make these gulping and burping sounds deep in their throats and then get their mouths so close it was like a third voice had joined in. It was such a weird sound. It filled the entire room with this thumping and gulping, and almost every time the women would start giggling and crack up and have to quit.

Nish couldn't help himself. "Sure hope they sell breath mints up here!" he shouted. Everyone laughed, but maybe they were just being polite.

Next came the competitions. They showed us all these amazing Arctic games. One was the blanket toss, where a group would gather around a blanket, holding the edges, and see who could toss a player highest while still making sure to catch them safely.

Another was called "Airplane," and you had to lie down on your stomach and stick out your arms and go stiff, like an iron cross, and three others would then pick you up by the arms and legs and carry you as far as you could go before you collapsed.

After they demonstrated the game, they invited the Owls to join in. Our best was Simon Milliken, which was a big surprise. Maybe because he's so light. Or maybe he's just a lot stronger than we know. Anyway, he went all rigid like an airplane, and Sam and Wilson and I carried him almost to the end of the hall before he gave out.

Nish, on the other hand, never even "took off." He went all rigid, but when Travis, Andy, and Fahd tried picking him up they couldn't move him. He collapsed before he even left the floor – though he denied it.

There was this one guy, this Inuit kid, who did it, and his team carried him all the way down the room and then all the way back again before he shouted something out to them and they put him down. It seemed he might have "flown" forever.

The kid got up, seemed to shake himself, almost like he was getting rid of some hard shell that had been wrapped around his body, and walked back into the applauding crowd without so much as a glance in anyone's direction.

Then they went around handing out loops of string and announced it was time for everyone to try the "ear pull." Lots of giggling with the Owls on that one.

Two young Inuit men demonstrated. They crouched together so their legs were nearly locked and then looped the string from the right ear of one to the left ear of the other. And then they started pulling.

It was so weird. Both were pulling hard, with the string cutting into their ears, yet the string held fast. Finally, the one guy pulled so hard he practically lifted the other guy out of his crouch. Very slowly the other guy rose up, and he almost did a flip before he screamed out and turned his head so the string could slip off his ear.

They got up, rubbed their ears, and congratulated each other, and everyone clapped for them — and then it was our turn.

I got Fahd. It was crazy. We were both laughing so hard we couldn't do it. I fell sideways finally, and the string broke free, and Fahd claimed he beat me. I didn't care. It was a good laugh.

After this, they cleared the centre of the room and everyone gathered around in a huge circle while they set up a pole that had a cross-piece on top with a string hanging down and a small fish carved out of wood tied to the end.

A very fit looking young man came in wearing a track suit and explained to the Governor General that this game was the "high kick," the most important competition in all the Arctic games.

They set up the high kick so that the little wooden fish was dangling just above the man's head. He stepped back, paced it out a couple of times, took a long hard breath, and then bounded forward and jumped, using just one leg. With the other leg, he kicked out, catching the fish full on and sending it spinning high above the pole before it dropped down, bouncing on the end of the string. Everyone in the building cheered.

Someone steadied the fish and they moved it higher. The man kicked again, and struck it perfectly. They cheered again, louder.

They had to bring out a chair to get the fish higher this time. It seemed impossible that this wiry little guy could get his *hand* that high, let along his *foot,* and yet with two steps, a single-leg bound, and a sharp, high kick, he struck it perfectly. And the next time. And the next. And each time the crowd cheered harder.

When he had gone what seemed to be at least twice his own height, he turned, bowed to the Governor General, and announced that anyone who wished to try was welcome to.

"Me!" shouted Nish.

"Me, too," said Sarah.

"I'll try," said Travis.

So I figured I'd try my luck too.

The fish was lowered to about chest height, and all the Owls and several of the villagers were lined up for a go at it. It was simple elimination. If you missed, you were out. If you hit, you stayed in.

Nish went first, whining that he'd turned his ankle playing golf, of all things, and couldn't jump as high as usual.

He missed straight away, the Owls all booing while the rest of the crowd gave him polite applause. Obviously, they don't know Nish.

I found it easy. The first several rounds, I got it no problem, and soon there were only five of us in the competition, including Sarah and me from the Owls. Now they gave us each two tries before they raised it higher.

Sarah missed on her second, and so did two of the local kids.

That left only the two of us – me and the kid who'd turned himself into an airplane. Unlike anyone else, he was doing this barefoot. He'd kicked the first few times with runners on, but later, when it got harder, he sat and removed his shoes and socks.

You could feel the crowd getting involved. It was sort of like being in a key hockey game, but without your team behind you. I couldn't count on Travis or Sarah getting me the puck, or Nish hitting me with one of his long hoist passes. Just me, all alone.

We both kicked, and hit, and they raised it higher still. It was now over my head.

What was really strange was that everyone in the hall was cheering for both of us. If I hit, they roared. If the other kid hit, they roared again. No favourites.

On the next kick, I missed, and he hit first time. On my second try, I barely ticked the fish, but it danced on the end of the string, enough to carry on.

I went first next time. Missed. Then missed again.

The other kid hadn't won yet – he still had to get it. But he asked for the fish to be raised even higher. He spread his hands to show how far. It wasn't just a bit – it was ten centimetres or more. I remember looking over at Sarah and how she rolled her eyes. And we thought *Nish* was a showboat!

And yet this kid never looked to one side or the other, never played to the crowd. Instead, he stepped back and seemed to go into a trance as bullet-proof as his trance when he turned himself into an airplane.

You couldn't hear a thing. No one was even breathing.

He stayed like that for what seemed a long time, then he took his two steps – you'd swear he was moving in slow motion – and sprang.

If he looked like an airplane before, it was nothing compared to now. He *took off* – rising so gracefully and high – and then, like the tongue of a rattlesnake, his foot snicked out and clipped the fish so hard it flew straight up and tore the string right off the pole.

The gasp that came from the crowd was amazing. Then, slowly, applause and cheering that just kept building.

The kid never even looked up. He picked up the jacket he had put on the ground, grabbed his runners and socks, and slipped into the crowd with his head down low.

"Who was that?" I asked one of the Inuit men.

"That?" the man practically giggled, as if he couldn't believe I didn't know. "That's Zebedee Okalik – the best hockey player Pang ever produced."

Muck Munro

THANKS BUT NO THANKS.
 The journals are for the kids.
 I already passed Grade Eight.

Fahd Noorizadeh

DATA AND I ARE GETTING GREAT MATERIAL. The village is a fascinating place, with the Cumberland Sound running alongside it and the mountains in the background. Everything looks so amazingly different when there are no trees and no grass. The homes are all small – too expensive to heat a big home, they say – but mostly well kept. There's even a sort of mall with a store and a special outlet for Inuit carvings and Pang knitwear. So we are getting video of the artists at work, too.

But today was Game One – and that meant Data was on his own, because, of course, I have to play.

It felt goofy getting back on skates after so long off. It's a great little rink, though, complete with artificial ice. It seems strange that you'd need artificial ice in the Arctic, but that's the way it is. They used to have outdoor natural ice, but when the long days began each spring there would be too much melting. So now the kids in the Arctic are just like kids in Florida – playing on artificial ice.

Muck didn't say much. Muck never says much. He just said to go out and enjoy ourselves.

Game One was against the local peewee team, the Pang Polar Bears.

Funny, isn't it, how warm-ups really tell you nothing. I can remember playing against teams where the kids all skated out with top-of-the-line equipment – composite sticks, NHL-quality gloves, matching socks and jerseys, super-expensive skates, "the whole shebang," as Mr. D. would say – and then we'd discover they could barely play the game. Then, on the opposite end, you'd have teams like the Kazakhstan Komets coming out, looking so rag-tag you'd think they'd fall down as soon as they hit the ice, and they'd leave you spinning with their speed and skill.

That's the way it was with the Polar Bears. Ever since the feast, we'd all been talking about this Zebedee character – Nish calls him Zip-a-Dee-Doo-Dah – and in the warm-up you wouldn't even notice him.

But then we played the game.

Muck started me with Nish on defence, and Sarah's line up front with Trav and Dmitri on the wings. First shift and it seemed we were away: Nish hit Dmitri with the long pass, and before you knew it Dmitri faked the goalie, went to his backhand, and blew the water bottle right off the top of the net.

What else is new?

It's a good thing they don't scout at the peewee level. If any team ever watched a video of Dmitri, they'd know what he was going to do. It's not his only move, but sometimes you'd think it was.

Anyway, we were up 3–0 and cruising along and this kid simply decided to take over the game all on his own.

Nish had been teasing him, even calling him Zip-a-Dee-Doo-Dah as the two teams lined up for the faceoff. Zebedee looks up, stares hard at Nish, smiles a big smile with a tooth missing, and that was it.

He beat Sarah on the draw. He spun with the puck and tucked it between my skates, then walked in and pulled Jeremy so far out of the net poor Jeremy may as well have been playing centre!

Bang! In off the crossbar. 3–1 Owls.

And he wasn't finished there, either. A few minutes later, he comes up over centre against Andy's line and suddenly slips into a new gear – almost like he's been shot from a cannon. He comes in on Sam and Wilson so fast that he blows right through them, splitting the defence and hammering a hard low shot that Jeremy missed with his glove.

"Zip-a-Dee-Doo-Dah tries that one again," Nish says to me on the bench, "we squeeze him out, okay? We *crush* Zippy, eh?"

"Sure," I said. It wasn't supposed to be a contact tournament, but you can always get away with some. And besides, when you're playing defence, you can just act like you got in the way.

It was 3–2 with only a minute or so left in the game when Sarah and Travis broke in on a two-on-one. Travis threaded a perfect pass to Sarah under the defenceman's stick, and Sarah one-timed her shot right off the post.

Dmitri tried for the rebound, but the puck bounced and his shot whiffed.

Zebedee had the puck, and he put himself into that extra gear and came charging fast up the ice, Nish and I backpedalling like crazy to cut him off. There was never any doubt what we'd do. He came across centre like a bullet and then our blue line, with the two of us just far enough apart that he figured he could split the defence again.

That's when Nish put his big butt in motion. We both moved to cut off his path, meeting perfectly just as the puck slid between our skates.

We hit him at the same time – dead on and hard. A penalty for sure, but it was worth it. I could hear Nish singing. I'm not kidding, *singing!*

"*Zip-a-dee-doo-dah, zip-a-dee-ay. My, oh, my, what a wonderful day.*"

I could feel Zebedee, half on my back, half on Nish's back, and then suddenly he does this spring thing and pulls off a complete somersault in the air, landing perfectly on his skates – and is in alone on Jeremy.

Nish and I crash together, both going down hard.

Quicker than either Nish or I can recover, the puck's so high in the net it's stuck in the mesh back of the inside bar. And Zebedee is coming back, smiling that gap-toothed smile – and *he's* singing!

"*Wonderful feeling, feeling this way!*"

I couldn't help it. I started laughing.

Nish, though, he didn't think it was funny at all. He cuffed me on the back of my helmet with his glove. I turned as if to say "What the – ?" and saw Nish was in no mood for singing or laughing. He was redder than the Screech Owls crest on his jersey.

Muck hauled us off and Nish just sat there, head between his knees. I didn't have to see his face to know he was scowling.

The game ended in a 3–3 tie and we started making our way from the bench to the dressing room. Nish was behind me, breathing hard. I could just make out what he said over the cheering of the crowd.

"I'm gonna get that guy," he said. "Gonna get him good."

8

Samantha Bennett

THIS JOURNAL IS THE PROPERTY OF SAM
Bennett.

So keep your sweaty hands off, Nishikawa!

What an idiot he is. We're guests here in this
unbelievable town, and what does Nish go and do?
He tries to knock their star player out of the hockey
tournament.

Smart move, Big Butt.

You should have heard him whining in the dressing room after the game. You'd think this kid had
stolen his lunch or something – well, he did fake
Nish out of his jockstrap, didn't he? – but Nish
wouldn't let up about how he was going to get even
with that fancy hotshot.

Sarah and I went over to the Pang dressing room
and waited for the team to come out so we could
shake their hands and congratulate them on a nice,
clean game. You'd hardly notice their big star off the

ice. On the ice, you can't take your eyes off Zebedee, but when he came out in a track suit, with his head down, you wouldn't even think he was a player. He's no bigger than anyone else, no heavier, and he's so shy you hardly get to see his face. I wouldn't even have known it was him if he hadn't looked up and smiled when Sarah spoke to him – he has enough teeth missing, Dmitri could roof a backhand into the top of his mouth.

"Hockey injury?" I asked.

"Brother," he said. "Slingshot."

Well, he doesn't talk much, but he makes himself understood.

"Love your team logo," Sarah said, pointing to the cartoon polar bear on his team jacket.

"Thanks," he said. "It's a polar bear."

"We know!" I said. "Sarah and I are mad for polar bears!"

"Have you ever seen one?" Sarah asked.

Zebedee looked up, less shy now, and he smiled again. "Many times," he said. "We have them here."

"Do you think we could see one?" I almost shouted. I must have been embarrassing. I was squealing like some little kid meeting a rock star.

Zebedee thought for a moment. "Not here," he said. "You only see them if you go out on the land ... or on the ice. My uncle is a hunter. He takes us out sometimes, and he shot one last year. My mom and I were with him."

My heart collapsed. "*Shot one?*"

Zebedee fixed me with eyes, black as hockey pucks. "He's a hunter," he said. "What do you expect him to do? Shoot pigs so we can have bacon?"

Sarah jumped in. "But they're protected, aren't they?"

Zebedee nodded. "You're right, from big-game hunters. People who just want to put a head on a wall. There's still a bit of that in the North, but I don't think it will last much longer.

"When I say hunter, I mean every person who lives in Pang. When my uncle gets a bear, everybody is involved. My mom skinned the last one right out on the land where it fell. We cut it up and brought it back here in two sleds. Then the whole village had a feast. They use every single bit of the fur to make boots and blankets. They use the oil. They use the bones to make tools for skinning the seals.

"No one values the life of the polar bear more than the hunter who has to kill him."

"We . . . understand," I said, even though I couldn't believe I was saying such a thing.

"How could we get to see a live polar bear?" Sarah said.

Zebedee thought for a moment.

"I'll ask my uncle."

Sarah and I had no idea what Zebedee would come up with, but it sounded promising. We liked this young guy who had lost his front teeth to his brother's slingshot. He was well spoken, and we didn't even realize he was talking in his second language until he started yelling at one of his teammates to wait up.

The rest of the Owls had already gone back to the community centre, where we were storing our hockey bags and sticks. The two of us started heading back, talking about our new friend along the way and wondering if there was any chance at all – oh please, please, *please* – that we might get to see a polar bear.

"What's this?" Sarah said, stopping in her tracks.

I looked ahead. There was a large gathering around the Royal Canadian Mounted Police station. There were snowmobiles and all-terrain vehicles and even the RCMP truck – though I had no idea what it was there for, since there were hardly any roads in Pang.

The crowd seemed excited about something. They were all pressing in tight to the two uniformed Mounties, who were staring down at something.

Sarah and I dropped our equipment and moved closer. Some of the men were hunters. They were carrying rifles, and one of the snowmobiles had a sled attached that was holding three bloodied seals.

We could smell the seals. It was strong enough to make you gag. But we pressed in.

The men were talking English and Inuktitut. We could only understand the English.

"How many of these did you find?" the one Mountie was asking an older hunter.

They were staring down at something the hunter had spread over the seat of the snowmobile. I got up on tippy-toe and could see what looked like shotgun shells and a couple of things that looked like darts.

The hunter was talking fast, part in English, part in Inuktitut.

"Blood . . . fur . . . more blood there . . ." and then he made hand signals to indicate a helicopter.

"Slow down! Slow down!" the second Mountie said. "Let's take this one step at a time."

The old hunter shut up and waited.

"You found these back of the basin?" the Mountie asked.

The hunter nodded.

"How many hours from here?"

The hunter thought, then held up three fingers.

The Mountie nodded. "Three hours." He picked up one of the shells and one of the darts. "These came from a tranquillizer gun," he said.

The other Mountie nodded, picking up another shell. "And the rifle was high calibre," he said. "A big gun. Big animal."

"But what about this blood?" the first Mountie said, looking confused.

The old hunter said nothing. He stepped back to his sled and untied a tarp, which he rolled back.

Sarah and I could hear the gasps.

I could see, just barely. White, white fur, and blood, smeared everywhere.

I burst into tears.

It was a baby polar bear. *Dead*.

Larry Ulmer

SOMETIMES I GET A LITTLE TIRED OF IT, YOU know. "Data, find this out!" "Data, get the details on this!" "Google it, Data – and let us know."

I am not a machine, but sometimes they treat me like one. I'm supposed to be assistant coach of the Screech Owls, but a lot of the time I'm looking up facts, facts that guys like Nish are too lazy to look up for themselves.

In a way, I don't mind. I'm good on computers. Fahd and I are far and away the most technical-minded of all the Owls. It's why we've been assigned to do the video work to go with the journals we all have to hand in at the end of this trip.

Fahd and I have been all over Pang videotaping. We spent time in the art studio watching Inuit carvers take a big hunk of green rock and, before the day was out, turn it into a dancing bear that would make you laugh just to look at it. We got video of the knitters who make the famous Pang hats that everyone has gone crazy for. They're more colourful than a kaleidoscope – and Sarah and Sam wear theirs everywhere. Even Mr. D. bought one, to cover up his bald head in the constant sunshine here.

We've done the village, too. Fahd pushes me, and as I wheel down the streets I get shots of the houses and the dogs and snowmobiles and boats and a few hunters' places where sealskins and Arctic fox pelts are stretched out for curing. We got some good footage of a very old lady skinning a beaver, too. Fascinating to watch how fast she worked with those funny curved knives. Fahd says they look a bit like hockey skates, and I can see where he gets that.

We got some great shots of airplanes taking off and landing on the gravel strip that pretty well runs through the centre of the village. We got down at the far end of the runway, and you could practically touch the wheels as the cargo planes took off.

We never expected to be shooting a dead polar bear cub, though.

Sarah and Sam came bursting into the room in tears, both of them screaming at us to get the camera and get down to the RCMP station.

By the time we got there, the little creature had been spread out on the ground and the Mounties were poking at it to see where it had been shot. It almost made me ill. Such a cute little thing, and the fur so brilliantly white, except where it was dark and matted with blood.

Now I'm assembling some facts on polar bears. Fortunately they have high-speed Internet here – actually, every community in Nunavut has it – and so I've been able to find what we need to know about these huge white bears.

- Male polar bears can weigh more than seven hundred kilograms and stand three metres tall – twice the size of females.
- They are the world's largest predators and have no natural enemies – apart from human hunters!
- There are as many as twenty-five thousand polar bears throughout the world. Two-thirds of them are found in Canada's North.
- Manitoba is the one Canadian province with polar bears that does not allow hunting.
- The territory of Nunavut sets a maximum number that can be hunted. Officials arrange it so more males than females will be hunted – and do not want cubs hunted at all.
- Polar bear "sport" hunting – unlike Inuit hunting, which is for food, and the skin, and so on – can be a huge international business. Wealthy big-game hunters have been known to spend over $500,000 to get a chance to shoot a prized polar bear.

- Polar bears travel constantly in search of food and need the Arctic ice to get around. A male bear can eat as much as forty-five kilograms of seal blubber in a day. Polar bears have even been known to attack and kill beluga whales. Polar bears are excellent swimmers. They do not hibernate in winter like other bears do.

- Scientists at the United States Geological Survey have predicted that by the year 2050, two-thirds of all polar bears will have disappeared because of climate change. The ice where the bears hunt will have mostly turned to water, so many will starve.

- In 2008, the American government listed the polar bear as a threatened species under the Endangered Species Act.

After I gathered together this material, the Owls met in a room at the community centre and I read out what I had learned.

"What does that mean?" Sam wanted to know when I'd finished the last point.

"It means Americans are no longer allowed to hunt polar bears," I explained.

"But they don't even have polar bears," Jenny argued.

"Not so," I told her. "Alaska has lots of polar

bears. That means no more hunting there. It's a big issue."

"Why would they hunt them anyway?" Simon asked.

"Big-game hunters," I explained. "A polar bear is considered a huge prize. Right up there with African lions."

"They don't eat them?" Sam asked.

"They stuff them," I said. "Or make a rug out of them. Or put their heads up on the wall. No, they don't eat them. There's a big difference between big-game hunters – they call them *sport* hunters – and the real hunters we see around here."

"Doesn't sound like sport to me at all," said Sam. "They should have another name for it. Like *killers*."

"If they can't hunt in Alaska," said Travis, "won't the big-game hunters just come here?"

"That's a whole other issue," I explained.

From what I could tell, some people thought the Canadian territories should welcome the sport hunters because they spent a lot of money, which was good for the local economy; others thought there should be a complete ban on sport hunting. One Web site said it no longer mattered, as the United States now had a ban on bringing polar bear skins into the country, which would put an end to sport hunting anyway. But a blogger on that site said this wasn't so. Half the world's big-game hunters aren't even American, he said, and European and Asian big-game hunters could still come to hunt polar bears.

I explained all this to the team as best I could, but I have to admit that even I was confused about how much polar bear "sport" hunting was actually taking place around the world.

Sarah seemed only interested in what had happened right here in Pang. "Why," she asked, "would *anyone* shoot a cub?"

"And if they shot it, why didn't they take it?" Andy added.

"Maybe they took something else," Rachel Highboy suggested.

Everyone turned and looked at Rachel. "What do you mean?" Wilson asked her.

"Well, think about it. The hunter found tranquillizer darts as well as shells, right?"

"Yeah."

"Well, I doubt very much that whoever shot the cub first tranquillized it so they could hit it more easily."

That made sense.

"So there must have been some other reason for the tranquillizer."

That, too, made sense. But I couldn't quite figure out how. "Like what?" I asked her.

"Maybe the cub got in the way, that's all."

"What do you *mean?*" Sam practically screamed.

"Maybe they wanted the mother bear."

"But only the cub was found." Sam said.

"Exactly," said Rachel. "So where did the mother end up?"

Rachel Highboy

I DO NOT KNOW IF ANYONE WILL EVER READ my "journal" or give me a mark – but I feel if I don't keep one, I won't be a full part of the team.

So here it is: Property of Rachel Highboy, Waskaganish, James Bay, Temporary Screech Owl, Forward.

This has already been the most amazing experience of my life. I thought *I* lived in the Far North, but it's all relative. We have trees where I come from – short ones, maybe, and only spruce, but still trees – and the water around my village has been open for weeks. Here, you can still walk out on the ice, for the most part. There's a channel where some boats come and go, and some of the ice floes are the size of icebergs, so you'd want to be careful. But some parts are frozen enough that they're snowmobiling across the bay, and I've even seen a couple of dog teams heading out with sleds.

Best of all is seeing my old friend Travis. He's grown a bit — no longer shorter than I am! We're almost exactly the same height now. And we get along as well as ever. I'm so glad we kept in touch after the Owls came to James Bay.

We played the Resolute Rebels this morning, and it wasn't nearly as good a game as we had against the Pang Polar Bears. Dmitri scored once again on his first shift, Sarah got two goals — one on a nice wraparound — and Andy, Nish, and I also scored for a 6–1 win.

Yes, you read it right. *I* scored. Okay, so it was a bit of a fluke. I was on a line with Derek and Andy, and Derek made a nice pass back to Sam, and Sam blasted a shot that went in off my rear end.

But you know what they say in hockey: they all count, even the ugly ones.

Sarah and Sam wanted to go out on the land — though often that means ice up here — and Zebedee came through with an offer from his Uncle Tagak. He would be checking one of his usual hunting routes, and we could go with him. Three extra snowmobiles were available, room for two people on each, and lunches were already packed. The entire trip would take maybe four hours.

Muck said yes. Mr. D. said yes. Since Zebedee had already asked on behalf of Sarah and Sam, they were automatically going. Mr. D. decided who would take the other three places by having the Owls pick numbers. I got lucky.

Uncle Tagak was in the lead snowmobile, pulling a sled with supplies, emergency equipment, and two rifles – one for safety, he told us, in case the first one jammed.

I could tell Sam and Sarah didn't like the guns, but I'm well used to them where I come from. In fact, I'd be far more nervous heading out *without* guns, to tell you the truth. But then, the Crees and Inuit don't see them as weapons. To us, they're tools, as important to my family of hunters as a tractor is to a farmer, or an office is to a banker.

Sam was running the second snowmobile, with Sarah on back. Travis picked a winning number and got the third – with *me* on back! And the final machine, which would run backup and be in charge of lookout, fell to Zebedee and his partner.

Nish.

No kidding, Nish. The guy who claimed he'd rather go to McDonald's. Who said there was nothing out there but ice anyway, so why bother going? Who said he already had more experience than any of the rest of the Owls with snowmobiles, so he'd have to drive.

I needn't explain, surely, why they put him back of Zebedee.

Nish seemed really peeved about that. One, he wasn't driving. And two, I don't think he likes Zebedee – probably because Zebedee made such a fool of him in our game against the Polar Bears.

I could see Zebedee grinning as Nish, his face beet red from humiliation, straddled the seat behind him. Zebedee has the greatest grin you ever saw – he's missing a bunch of teeth, which makes him look like one of those old-time hockey players from the black-and-white photos!

Off we went, at first slowly, while Sarah and Travis got a feel for driving the snowmobiles, then faster and faster as Uncle Tagak picked up the pace. I could feel the wind in my face, and every once in a while air would cup in the sides of my helmet and the wind would roar. There were times when it drowned out the roar of the engine.

We flew across the bay along a well-worn route, Zebedee's uncle darting between massive walls of ice and dropping off jumps and at times even skipping fast across what appeared to be open water – but wasn't.

So beautiful. If you looked down and the sun was out, you could see blues and greens and even a nearly fluorescent green-blue – aqua, I guess you'd call it. The effect has to do with the depth of ice and layers of water trapped at various levels. The colours were exquisite.

Zebedee's uncle pulled over up ahead and raised an arm to tell us to stop and be quiet. Travis brought our machine to a halt. Uncle Tagak walked quietly to a large ice block, at least five times as tall as he was, and peered around the corner. He had one of the rifles in his arms.

He waved us all forward, and one by one, as we crept up to the ice block, we leaned out and looked at what he was pointing toward.

There was a small dark hole ahead in the ice, and lying beside the hole was a large, fat seal. It was almost as if he was sunning! All he needed was some sunscreen, a pair of sunglasses, and a book, and he'd look like he was at the beach.

"Cute," whispered Sam.

"Not cute," corrected Uncle Tagak. "Food."

"Ring seal," said Zebedee. "My favourite."

Zebedee's uncle handed him the rifle. "You shoot."

I could hear Sam and Sarah gasp. Both of them turned white, like they were in shock. But what did they *think* was going to happen? That Uncle Tagak was going to stand guard over the seal in case a hungry old polar bear came along?

Zebedee nodded and took the rifle. He stepped out from the cover of the ice block and squatted, aiming at the seal.

"You're not —" Sam started.

Uncle Tagak answered by placing a big hand tight over Sam's mouth.

Zebedee aimed, looked up to see if there was any wind, looked down again through the sights – and fired. The sound cracked across the ice and bounced back in echoes all over the bay. The seal seemed to jump, once, straight up in the air, then rolled and went still. "Good shot!" Uncle Tagak called.

"You killed him!" Sam screamed when Zebedee's uncle took his hand away.

"I shot him!" Zebedee replied, sternly but calmly. "He will feed our family. Do you eat meat?"

Sam figured she had him. "Not red meat."

Zebedee smiled. "So you think fish and chicken aren't alive?"

"No . . . no," she sputtered.

"This is our garden," Zebedee said. "Think of it that way. And if we don't take care of our garden – if we over-hunt or just kill because we see something we can shoot – we will destroy our garden and destroy ourselves."

Sam said nothing.

"It's easy to judge when you aren't living here," he said. "But you've been around the village. See any carrots growing? Or potatoes? Peas? Corn?"

Sam shook her head.

"See any chickens?"

She shook her head.

"Then you understand," Zebedee said, smiling to soften the lecture. Sam nodded. Not happily, but she nodded.

We went by snowmobile to collect the seal, which was very much dead, fortunately, by the time we arrived. Uncle Tagak wrapped it in a tarp and packed it tightly into the back of the sled. And we were off again.

You could tell when you left the ice and hit solid ground. We went up an incline and suddenly the roar of the treads was entirely different. It might look the same, but it sure doesn't sound the same. We had crossed the bay.

The trail began to twist and turn more, and rise and fall. We were going along quite happily, with a rise ahead of us, when suddenly Zebedee's snowmobile flew by up the hill at twice the speed anyone else was going. Even over the awful roar of Zebedee's machine at full throttle, we could hear Nish on the back.

"HELP MMMMMEEEEEE!!!"

It looked as if Zebedee was going to smash his machine straight into a hard curl of solid ice that hung out from the crest of the hill.

Up they roared, with the rest of us now screaming, and we watched as Zebedee crashed into the curl of white. Snow exploded harmlessly all around the machine – it wasn't ice at all, but snow that had been shaped by the wind. There was a hole where Zebedee and Nish had blown right through.

By the time we made it up and over the hill, Zebedee had got off the machine and was laughing so hard he was rolling around on the ground.

Nish was standing to the side, white as a sheet. He was furious.

"I won't forget!" he said angrily to Zebedee.

Nor would the rest of us! We were all laughing so hard it made Nish even madder. He stomped so hard, if we'd still been on the ice we'd probably now be at the bottom of the Arctic Ocean.

Uncle Tagak pulled away to head higher into the hills, and we quickly followed him. We rose high into plateaus where there was still snow on the ground, and we crossed creeks and pushed through gravel-like ground coming up through the melting snow.

We headed higher and higher until, finally, Uncle Tagak pulled over and got off his snowmobile. He began walking over to the edge of the cliff, and signalled for us to follow.

When we got there, it took our breath away. It seemed we could see forever.

The sea stretched out in front of us, and floating everywhere were huge icebergs of brilliant white, green, blue, turquoise, aqua – unbelievable colours in the twenty-four-hour sunlight.

Uncle Tagak began speaking fast to Zebedee, and Zebedee translated for us.

"Uncle says the water has never been as open as this," Zebedee said. "What you are looking at is the famous Northwest Passage, the route to China sought by every explorer from as early as Champlain. . . . Usually, much more of it is frozen. No one living in Pang has ever seen it so open as it is right now. . . . Any other year it would be September before it opened at all, and maybe not even then. . . . My uncle is very worried."

"What about?" asked Sarah.

"If the ice melts much more, he will not be able to hunt," Zebedee explained. "He will not be able to find the seals. And if the bears can't reach the seals because there's no ice for them to travel on, the bears will starve. And if the bears vanish, the people may as well leave, too. Uncle says he has met people who have seen birds never before seen in the North. And bees."

"Bees?"

"Yes, bees."

"You don't have any here?"

"Never have had. But they say they've been seen."

Uncle Tagak spoke in English. "Look," he said, pointing off into the distance. I could make out a red blur.

"It's a ship," said Zebedee. "We would never see a big ship here in June before. Never."

Uncle Tagak had his binoculars out. He handed them to Zebedee, who took a look and then handed them to me. It was a large ship and seemed to have a special landing platform on it. But I couldn't be sure.

"Coast Guard?" Zebedee asked.

Uncle Tagak shook his head. "Not Canada," he said. "Something else."

We were all taking turns looking and then – in an instant – we were all flat on our stomachs. Someone screamed. I couldn't tell if it was Sarah or Nish or Sam or Travis – or all four of them.

How it happened so fast, I don't know, but suddenly there was this enormous roar and then wind pounded down on us like hammers. A helicopter! It must have been flying very low, because it just leapt up out of the valley we'd been travelling through. It felt like it had almost hit us.

The chopper roared past, and we all looked up to watch. It was trailing something large, a huge box of some sort attached to the helicopter by cables. From our vantage point it looked empty, but it was difficult to say.

Then the helicopter turned around. It was the weirdest thing – almost like it was an animal that had caught our scent and was turning back on us.

It roared back and settled overhead, the big rotor making this *whup-whup-whup-whup* sound as it steadied and dropped down closer. I could see the side panels open, and a man was sitting there with binoculars trained on us.

"It's that guy!" Travis shouted at Nish.

"It is, too."

"The helicopter at the golf course!" shouted Sarah.

Uncle Tagak raised his binoculars to get a better look, but then, just as quickly as it had turned and come back, it turned the other way and shot off.

We watched it go, out over the open ocean, and then come around into the wind to approach the ship. It settled down on the landing platform. But it was too far away to see how many people were there or what they were unloading.

"Scientists," said Travis.

"I don't think so," said Zebedee. "We're used to scientists. It's hard to imagine a pilot not tipping his wings to us or waving. They looked like they were teed off that we were here – like we were trespassing or something! Except, how can we trespass on our own land? *They* are the trespassers!"

"That guy sure didn't look very friendly," said Sarah.

"He gave me the creeps," added Sam.

By the time we were heading back, the light had changed. Shifted, sort of. The sun wasn't going down – it wouldn't go down at all – but it did travel across the sky and now the shadows were longer and bluer from the ice walls along the trail back.

Everyone was taking it easy and was well stretched out. We could barely see Uncle Tagak up ahead. And how far back Zebedee and Nish were was anyone's guess.

I don't really even know how it happened, but Travis was guiding our snowmobile around a block and suddenly we were face to face with a huge polar bear! He was standing there, his head bobbing oddly.

Travis made a spluttering noise, like he was being strangled. *"What do I do?"* was he all managed to say.

The bear stood up on its hind legs, sniffing. It towered above us! The biggest bear I have ever seen – or even imagined. I thought my heart was going to pop right through the top of my head.

"Hit it!" I shouted.

"The bear?"

"No! No! No! The gas! Get outta here!"

Travis squeezed hard on the accelerator and the machine bolted off to the side. But now the bear was charging!

Travis had swerved off track and was trying to hold the machine steady – I was terrified we were going to flip – and the bear was moving as fast, no faster, than us.

"*Turn back!*" I screamed.

Travis did – both of us leaning hard in the direction of the turn. The snowmobile held its grip, both skis stayed down, and we turned just as the bear shot by. He was so close I could smell him.

Travis goosed the gas and we shot back in the direction we had just come from, the bear turning fast and chasing after us.

And that's when we heard Nish's scream again.

"HELLPP!"

Zebedee was coming toward us at a dangerous speed, his snowmobile at full throttle – he could flip his machine if he hit so much as a piece of ice.

With Nish screaming behind him, Zebedee cut off the animal's charge, causing the big bear to spin in its tracks and now head off after Zebedee and Nish.

"HELLLLLPPPPPPPPP!!!!!!!"

Then came that frightening crack again, that ear shattering, echoing sound of Uncle Tagak's rifle. The bear stopped, just as if it had run into a stone wall. It buckled, rolled, then came up charging again, straight at Uncle Tagak, who was crouching down beside his snowmobile.

He was waiting for the perfect shot.

"*Shoot! Shoooot! Shoooooooot!*" Travis was yelling.

But Zebedee's uncle just waited.

Finally, with the bear so close it seemed Uncle Tagak might reach out and tap it on the nose with the rifle, he shot. The big bear went down head first, sliding on the sand and ice – dead before he landed.

We raced over, some of us in tears. All of us shaking.

Uncle Tagak was already checking the bear over. He didn't seem excited. He didn't seem frightened. He seemed concerned. He was looking at something wrapped around the big bear's foreleg. It looked like shredded, broken ropes.

"Someone tried to net this big guy," he said.

He used his foot to heave the bear over slightly. There was blood on him, and not just from the two shots that Uncle Tagak had taken.

There were two darts still stuck in his coat. Uncle Tagak pulled one out and examined it. "Tranquillizer gun," he said. He looked back in the direction we had just come from. Back toward the cliff where we had all stood staring out over the open sea at the mysterious ship.

Back toward the cliff where the helicopter had terrified us.

Without anyone saying a word, we all knew there had to be a connection.

Gordie Griffiths

I'VE NEVER BEEN VERY GOOD AT WRITING assignments, but Mr. D. says if I don't complete this we may never be able to take another trip in term time. So I'll do my best.

You should have seen the excitement when the kids came back from their snowmobile outing. We were all gathered down at the shore to greet them, because even when they were still way out on the ice we could see they were coming. They looked like black ants moving on the ice – perfectly trailing each other – but eventually we could see who was who, and then some of the Inuit kids started screaming when they caught sight of the hunter's sled.

"Bear!"

"BEAR!"

"BEAR!!!"

That got the rest of the village down, and by the time the snowmobiles reached the shore there must have been a crowd of two hundred or more. Even the Mounties were on their way down in their four-wheel drive, lights flashing like they were heading off to a traffic accident or something.

The Owls who were on the trip were talking so fast I'd have needed a tape recorder I could play back on "slow" if I was going to write it all down. Sam was sobbing. Sarah was half in tears and babbling. Travis was shaking like a leaf. He claimed – *ha!* – that it was because he'd been driving and the wind was cold.

Nish was telling everyone who would listen that he and the other kid – the one he was calling Zippy just the other day – had saved Travis's and Rachel's lives by cutting off the charging bear and giving Zebedee's uncle time to shoot.

When the Mounties got there they took down the story in their notebooks and then carefully checked out the big bear. Several of the men from Pang had turned down the sides of the sled and rolled him out onto a tarp they spread on the ground. They were all crouching down and examining the bear like they were doctors and the bear was in for a physical.

The police kept looking at each other. It seemed they wanted to take over – talk about "tampering with evidence" – but neither had the nerve to tell the hunters to step back. After all, who would know more about bears than the hunters?

The younger Mountie went to their vehicle and came back with a camera. Following the directions of the older Mountie, with the help of Zebedee's uncle, he began taking photographs of various parts of the animal.

There was one funny dart-like thing hanging from the bear and several wounds that looked like he'd been shot, but I couldn't tell you who had caused which ones. What I can tell you is that the two Mounties were very serious and seemed both upset and confused at the same time. The one Mountie kept asking Zebedee's uncle how many shots he had taken at the bear. Then he asked each of the kids the same question, over and over, almost as if he was trying to trip them up or something. It was very strange.

I really had no idea what was going on. And no one explained anything, either.

Finally, Mr. D. comes along and tells us all to head off to the community centre to grab our equipment. We'd absolutely forgot we had a game!

Simon Milliken

NISH SAYS I'M NOT TO USE ANY "BIG" WORDS —
what a funny, funny jerk he can be. What am I supposed to say to him? Don't use any "fat" words?
Don't say anything "stupid"? What else can he do?

Okay, my report is on Game Three of the 24/7
Sunlight Festival hockey tournament, Screech Owls
vs. the Iqaluit Ice Dogs. Night game — but you'd
never know it.

Finally we got a look at the so-called top team of
the tournament. Iqaluit is the capital of Nunavut, and
comparing Iqaluit to Resolute or Pang is like comparing Toronto or Montreal to Tamarack. We
changed planes there on the way up, and they have
paved roads, hotels, stores, a big airport, cars and
trucks, and buildings more than one storey high —
which is a lot more than can be said about little Pang.

The Ice Dogs have hundreds of kids to choose
from, whereas the Pang Polar Bears pretty much have

to take whatever kids are in town. If they didn't have Zebedee and a not-half-bad goalie, they wouldn't have much at all – though they tied us when I would have thought, from the warm-up, that we'd win by ten goals. You just never know in hockey.

The Ice Dogs looked good from the moment they raced out onto the ice with warrior shouts from each player as he or she hit the ice. Kind of neat. And their fans in the crowd shouted with them. Wish we'd thought of that.

I can't believe how many people come to watch the games. I can't be sure, but I'd be shocked if there was a single person on the streets of Pang while the tournament was on. One of the Mounties was even in the stands, careful to cheer for both sides at the same time, which must be hard.

The Pang team all sat together. They wore blue windbreakers with a small polar bear crest on the chest and the player's number on the arm. They were all sitting around Zebedee like he was the star, but he sure doesn't act like a star. He's polite and shy and hardly says a word.

Nish could take some lessons.

Speaking of Nish, it seemed he was determined to put on a special show with so many in the crowd and with Zebedee – the guy who made a fool of him in the first game – watching with his teammates.

The first time Nish touched the puck, it looked like he was going to play keepaway with it until he could dart out the far door and run right out of the arena with it. I have to admit, it was quite a display.

He picked the puck up behind his own net, came up along the boards on the right, where I was waiting for a pass, and then made it look like he was going to fire a pass across ice to Rachel, who was playing the other wing.

But instead he tried that crazy "spinnerama" move he's been fiddling with in practice. He fakes the pass, then spins backwards in the other direction, turning right around to face our goalie, then the boards, then continuing the spin with the puck on his backhand until he's moving past his checker and flying down the ice again. When it works, it's breathtaking. When it doesn't work, it's embarrassing.

This time it worked. Nish spun, the checker fell for the fake to Rachel, and Nish took off.

I was behind him – the forward following up on his own rushing defenceman – and I figured I'd better be careful to stay back and cover for Nish if he lost the puck.

Nish moved up over centre and hit the blue line, niftily banking the puck off the boards as he slipped around the inside of the defender. It was like he was passing to himself – and it worked wonderfully.

In two sneaky moves, Nish was in, nothing between him and the goal, if he could just use his size to protect the puck and drive his way to the front of the net for a cleaner shot.

Nish leaned into the other defender, let the puck drop into his own skates, and then delivered a third surprise by kicking the puck backwards while he sort of "accidentally" took out the defence.

Rachel had the puck now, and nothing between her and the net but air. She dropped a shoulder, faked once, went to the backhand, and slipped the puck in under the goalie's five-hole.

A true beauty. Highlight-reel quality. Brilliant. The only thing wrong with it was Nish had done it all and, of course, was instantly insufferable.

What else is new?

With Nish bragging on the bench that he was unstoppable, the Ice Dogs tied it up when Fahd lost the puck in his own end and they scored on Jenny off a scramble.

By the third period, the two teams were tied 3–3. Besides Rachel, Travis had scored on a sweet setup from Sarah and Dmitri, and Nish had scored on a hard shot from the point that the Iqaluit goalie had to have been screened on.

There were five minutes left in the game when Mr. D. began bobbing down the length of the bench letting us all know what was at stake. "We need the win, Owls," he said. "We don't want to end the round robin with two ties. We might be left out of the final."

Next shift, I was out, with Sam and Wilson back on defence, and it seemed Sam was going to do it all herself. She picked the puck up in her own end, fired a hard pass over to Wilson, and then broke up the side. Wilson saw her and hit her in the skates with a pass – but Sam was smart enough to turn her skate so that the puck struck the blade and skipped perfectly ahead to her stick, where she gathered it in and hit centre ice.

The Ice Dogs' centre was waiting and stabbed for the check, but Sam did her cute little tuck and just moved the puck out of the centre's reach. She was around the checker and in, with only the defence back and me and Rachel – (or should that be "Rachel and I"?) – moving up with her.

Sam hit Rachel with a nice pass and was still driving for the net, so I slowed and looped across the ice, hoping to set up the triangle for a nice tic-tac-toe. If Rachel dropped to me, I intended to pass immediately to Sam for the tap in.

Rachel dropped and I passed without first cupping the puck – *a mistake!* I heeled the puck and it shot slightly off to the side and lame, with Sam unable to reach back for it.

The Ice Dogs' defender picked up the loose puck and dashed away. Sam was gong the wrong way, and

I turned, but fell, and by the time I got up the Dogs were in on a three-on-one, with only Wilson back.

I raced back as hard as I could. The Dogs were separating to set up a triangle, and I guessed there would be a drop pass and then the high player would try and set up for a tap in on the side of the net.

So I took a chance. Instead of checking the player closest to me, I let the high player go and headed for the player stationing himself on the side of our net.

The Dog carrying the puck dropped it back to the player now in the high slot, as I figured he would, and the high player had obviously decided to do exactly what I had just tried at the other end of the ice – only this time the one-timer pass worked perfectly.

I dove, thrusting my stick out to try and block the pass. The puck hit my stick, bounced over it, and the player waiting for the pass swiped as hard as he could.

The puck was still in the air, fortunately, and he sort of "skyed" it, the puck ticking just off the cross bar.

Wilson gathered the puck and fired it back down the ice.

I was still getting up when I realized Jenny in goal was slamming her stick on the ice and yelling at me. "Way to go, Simon – great check!"

I never said a word. If she only knew that I had caused the near-goal myself.

Bailing her out was the least I could do.

There wasn't much time left.

Still 3–3 and Sarah's line was double shifting, with my own line sitting it out. It's okay. I understand. We needed the win, and why wouldn't Muck go with his best line in the final moments?

Sarah was back in our own end, digging in the corner for the puck and coming up with it even with two Ice Dogs on her.

She fired a hard, high pass around the boards and Dmitri brilliantly picked it out of the air with the blade of his stick. He hit Travis, who was cutting fast across centre.

Travis is a lovely puckhandler, and he stick-handled into the Ice Dogs end, looping back just as he got inside and waiting for his linemates.

He faked to Sarah, who drew one of the Dogs into the corner with her.

He faked again to Dmitri, who was heading for the other side of the net, and Dmitri managed to take another defender off into the corner.

Travis then flipped a saucer pass that seemed to land in the middle of nowhere – but he had timed it perfectly, and it was waiting there when big Nish came thundering over the blue line.

Nish gobbled up the puck, moved in on the one player standing between him and the net, and faked a pass back to Dmitri, coming back out of the corner. And then he did the spinnerama again, moving the puck to the back of his blade and spinning right around backwards as he continued moving toward the net.

The play so stunned the defender that the little guy fell to the ice.

Nish was in alone. He faked forehand, then went to his backhand, delayed long enough for the goalie to slide out of position – and promptly roofed a "Dmitri Special" into the net, the water bottle flying so high it hit, and splashed, against the glass back of the net.

You would think Nish had scored the Stanley Cup winning goal in the fifteenth overtime period. He jumped and hit the glass harder than the water bottle and then collapsed, lying there like he was just waiting for everyone to pile onto him – which of course we all did.

But I did think to look up into the stands before I joined in. I looked up to see how the Pang Polar Bears were reacting.

Zebedee was standing, holding his hand over his head like a ballerina, and spinning like he was dancing in *The Nutcracker.* And he and all his team-mates were howling with laughter.

Laughing at Nish.

Samantha Bennett and
Sarah Cuthbertson

WE ARE GOING TO DO THIS SECTION TOGETHER, as it concerns our special project on polar bears.

It all began with a knock on the door.

When we came here to Pangnirtung, we had this ridiculous idea that just maybe, with a bit of luck, we'd see a polar bear from a distance and get some good photographs of it with Sam's telephoto lens. We might even, with a lot of luck, manage to see a cub or two and get some photos of them playing.

How naïve we were.

Little did we know we'd have shots of polar bear cubs all right, but they'd be dead, killed for no reason at all that we could understand.

We were at our billets' home when the knock came. Sam was napping and Sarah was surfing the net in search of more scientific background on polar bears.

We were both tired from the hockey game – which was a pretty neat victory for the Owls, even if it did mean we all had to act like we were happy for the dreaded Nishikawa.

We thought it was one of the kids, Billy, calling us for dinner. But no, it wasn't Billy at all. It was Zebedee. And he had his finger raised to his lips so we'd keep quiet. He spoke in a whisper. "Can we go for a walk?" he said. "I need to talk to you two."

We looked at each other, wondering what was up, and then quickly put our shoes on and headed out into the brilliant late-evening sunlight. (We know. We'll never get used to it. It just seems insane to always be in the middle of the day here!)

We walked down along the water. Zebedee did most of the talking.

"I know about your polar bear project," he told us. "Everybody does. I think it's great."

But what had he come to see us about? Hardly to ask what the average weight of a male polar bear was. He would know a million times more about polar bears than we ever will.

"I want to check something out," he said. "But it's dangerous to go out onto the ice alone at this time of year. I can borrow my uncle's snowmobiles, and my mom has her own. If I can put something together, would you two be willing to come along?"

"What for?" Sam asked.

"I want to check out that ship."

We looked at Zebedee and then at each other. Nothing more needed to be said. Ever since the helicopter sighting and the two dead polar bears, we'd been talking about little else. Not even hockey could distract us. We just knew, deep down, that the ship and the helicopter were connected to the dead bear cub and the tranquillizer darts. But, of course, we could prove nothing.

"Count us in," Sarah said.

Zebedee nodded matter-of-factly, as if he had known all along we would join him.

"We need three more," he said. "Four more if my mom agrees to come along. I can drive one of my uncle's machines, and he has two others we can use. I'd like someone with experience driving on the ice. It can be very dangerous out there. Who would be most experienced of the Owls when it comes to the North and running a snowmobile?"

We both knew at once. "The Highboys," we said simultaneously. "Jesse and Rachel."

Zebedee nodded again, almost as if expecting that. "We also need someone who's small enough to sneak onto the ship, but strong enough to pull himself up or down if he has to."

Again, we didn't miss a beat. "Travis."

"And if my mom comes – one more can go. Maybe someone strong, in case we have to hoist our little spy up."

There was only one right choice – even if both of us dreaded the thought.

"Nish . . . ?" we said.

Zebedee nodded. "That's what I thought."

Jesse Highboy

I HOPE THIS ISN'T THE LAST THING I EVER write. Actually, I'm not writing it – not technically – I am speaking into this tiny recorder Data loaned me as we get ready to head off on this insane "mission" that this Zebedee character has come up with.

Sarah and Sam seem gaga about this Inuit kid with the hole in his teeth. He's a heck of a hockey player – much better than me, and maybe the equal of Sarah – but I have no idea what he's like out on the land. If our grandfather knew Rachel and I were heading out by snowmobile onto the barrens, I don't know what he'd say. But Rachel seems as thunderstruck by this kid's goofy smile as the other two girls are.

Nish being here surprised me. He doesn't even seem to like this Zebedee kid, but there he is, zipping himself into a snowmobile suit.

I'm just glad Travis is coming along. He's got a steady head. He's always good when there's trouble. And I smell trouble.

We set out after we were around the first curve in the shore. Zebedee acted like he was just giving us lessons – good grief, Rachel and I have been on snowmobiles since we were babies – but this was just a cover. Once we were out of sight, Zebedee and his mother – she says we should call her Annie – hooked on a couple of sleds with extra fuel and a couple of rifles. At least they knew what to bring. Once I saw the carefully packed sleds waiting for us, with their tents and tarps and fur and gas cans, I had a lot more faith in Zebedee.

Zebedee's mom is nice. She doesn't speak a great deal of English, but enough that we understand her. She reminds me of my grandparents, who understand English quite well but would prefer not to have to speak it. They're just more comfortable in Cree. Same with Zebedee's mom in Inuktitut.

Zebedee led us out onto the ice, our three snowmobiles following him like we were elephants joined trunk-to-tail in a parade. It's the safest way. You cover exactly the same track, and you stay just far enough apart that if one machine goes through, the others have time and space to stop and help. I checked back in the sled and there was strong nylon rope for hauling out and even a couple of good poles if one of us happened to go down with the machine. Let's hope not.

It was tough holding the snowmobile steady at times, especially when we were going over old broken ice that lay along the trail like boulders. And because of the open water we had to take several detours. But Zebedee seemed to know what he was doing.

We hit the far shoreline after about an hour and began the long climb up the hill to where the girls said they had spotted the ship when they were out with Zebedee's uncle. The climbing got tougher. Fortunately, all three machines were very powerful – the slightest pull on the gas lever and they would practically leap up the hill. You just had to be careful not to tip right over backwards. If a snowmobile rolls over you, you're likely dead – especially way out here in the middle of nowhere.

We drove in silence. With the roar of the machines, there was no use talking. I couldn't hear Travis behind me, but he's pretty quiet anyway.

Up ahead, Zebedee pulled over, and he and Sam got off the machine. He signalled for us all to hold up and for everyone to get off. There was still some hill to go.

Smart move. If someone was watching, they might notice a burst of exhaust if we needed to gun the engines to make it to the top. Or they might see us moving along the ridge.

We crept on foot up to the top and then fell on our bellies for the final upward wiggle and crawl. Zebedee and Annie reached the peak first and waved us up to join them.

It was my first sighting of the ship. It seemed tiny at such a distance, but the air was clean and clear and I could see much farther here than I ever could back in a place like Tamarack.

Zebedee had binoculars out and was scanning the terrain. He handed them around and we all checked it out.

"*Down!*" Zebedee suddenly shouted.

We were already down, but we crouched still lower. I could hear a dull roar, then the telltale *whup-whup-whup* of a helicopter in the distance.

We looked off toward the sound. It was far enough away it seemed small as a blackfly walking across a white wall.

"They won't see us," Zebedee said, rising slightly to watch with his binoculars. "They're coming in from the east."

We watched it come into closer range and saw that hanging below it, on cables, was some sort of steel box.

"It's going much slower than last time," said Sam.

"They're carrying a load," said Annie.

Everyone agreed that she was right. The box hung straight down, no slack at all in the cables.

"Let's get closer," said Zebedee. "All their attention will be on landing that thing safely."

We got back on our snowmobiles and Zebedee led the way down the spine of the hill, well out of sight, and then out onto the ice in the direction of the ship. It was like moving on a giant chessboard, with small icebergs spread out across it serving as the chessmen. They'd been formed by the shifting ice pack, and though they made travel more difficult, they also made it possible to sneak forward without being seen. We slipped along between them like four chipmunks chasing each other through a woodshed.

We couldn't see the ship from down among the blocks of ice, and the helicopter sound had vanished, meaning it must have landed. So I was stunned – and more than a little scared – when I realized how close Zebedee had taken us to the ship.

We rounded the corner of an ice block the size of a garage and suddenly there it was. You never saw such a quick turnaround as we executed on those machines! We all slipped back in behind the ice, dismounted, and crawled to the corner for a look.

The ship was large but not the size of an ocean freighter. It was anchored next to thick ice cover. A ramp had been lowered onto the ice, and three snowmobiles were parked at the bottom. The snowmobiles were connected to packed sleds. It seemed as if an expedition of some kind was about to depart.

The wind was blowing our direction, and every now and then we heard shouts and snippets of conversation. But we couldn't really make out anything that was being said.

Then the helicopter fired up again, the rotor starting slow, then picking up speed.

"*What's happening?*" Nish hissed in Zebedee's direction.

"Sounds like they're taking off," Zebedee said. "Everybody take cover!"

The helicopter rose straight up from the ship, cables still attached to the steel box, and it roared away fast in the direction it had come from. Away from us, mercifully.

The box hung quite loosely from the cables now, almost bouncing in the air, and the helicopter was moving away twice as quickly as it arrived.

"Whatever was in that box," said Travis, "they emptied it out. There's nothing in it now."

"They've gone for another load," said Sam.

We turned toward her, wondering how she would know.

Sam shrugged. "It stands to reason. They come in with a loaded box, drop off something, and immediately head out again. They must be moving something big."

"*Look!*" shouted Rachel.

Several figures in snowmobile suits were coming down the ramp from the ship. There were six of them, two for each of the snowmobiles hooked up down below. And they were all carrying rifles!

When they reached the bottom, they signalled to a lone figure at the top, who waved back and then cranked up the ramp part way – high enough that nothing, like a wandering polar bear, could come on board. With the ramp raised to a safe position, the man locked the crank and vanished from sight.

The six snowmobilers stowed their weapons and mounted their machines, quickly firing them up.

"What if they come this way?" Sarah said, fear in her voice.

"I don't think they will," said Zebedee.

He was right. They roared their engines a few times and then the lead snowmobile started off, fast, in the direction the helicopter had flown. The two others followed close behind.

"An accident waiting to happen," said a disgusted Annie.

What a contrast to the cautious, ants-in-a-line style of the Inuit, I thought. Those snowmobilers from the ship acted like the visitors we get at James Bay. They think the frozen ice is like some smooth, solid skating rink for them to play on.

Sometimes it is. Sometimes it isn't. And it doesn't take much for a small mishap to turn into a tragedy. One of the elders at the banquet told us a story about a hunter whose only mistake was to put his sealskin-lined glove down while he tied a knot in his dogsled line. A gust of wind had killed that man, the elder said. We couldn't understand how until he explained: the wind blew away the hunter's glove, his hand froze, and soon enough his life had been lost.

"What now?" said Rachel.

We all looked at each other.

"We don't know what they're doing on that ship," said Sarah.

"We can tell the Mounties they've got rifles," said Sam.

Zebedee smiled. "You won't find anyone out here *without* a rifle," he said, "not unless they're fools."

"What do we do, then?" asked Sam. "We all know something bad is happening here. The Mounties know about the tranquillizer guns."

Annie shook her head. "Lots of scientists use them," she said. "They might have been tagging those bears and just got in a bad situation. It happens. We don't know."

"But we *do* know," said Sarah, "that these guys are up to no good here."

Annie nodded in agreement.

Zebedee opened up his pack. He rummaged around and came out with a camera bag. "We can get photographic evidence," he suggested.

"Of the ship?" I asked.

"Of the helicopter when it comes back?" Travis asked.

Zebedee shook his head. "No. We'll have to get on board somehow. We'll need proof of whatever it is they're up to."

"Whatever it is," said Rachel, "it's no good."

Whatever it is, I said silently to myself, it's dangerous.

I did not have a good feeling about this.

Travis Lindsay

I JUST HOPE THIS ISN'T MY LAST WILL AND
testament . . .

Jesse has been handing off Data's little recorder to
me every so often, and I've had a few moments
to put down some "journal" thoughts – but it's difficult to think about school assignments when you
feel like your life is on the line.

Zebedee and Annie ran ahead to scout out the
ship and its raised ramp. For the first time since we
got here, I'm wishing we didn't have twenty-four-
hour sunlight. We could do with a little cover of
darkness about now. They were gone about twenty
minutes before they came scrambling back over the
ice chunks. It had been rough going, as sweat was
pouring off both their faces. Zebedee took a few
moments to catch his breath.

"The ship is right up against a solid ice floe," he said
finally. "It's anchored pretty solid. It's hard to say if the

ramp has been raised to keep anyone – or any*thing* – from coming aboard or from getting off. My mom thinks maybe both. I don't know. I can't figure it out.

"Near as we could make out, there is only that one guy on board. Maybe there's two or three, but no more. We never saw any sign of anyone. It appears he just winched up the ramp and then went straight inside."

"What do you suggest we do?" Sarah asked.

Zebedee looked at Annie. "What do you think, Mom? Should we try and get on board?"

Annie looked concerned. "I can't see that we have any choice," she said. "You go back to the RCMP with photos of a ship, they're going to laugh at you. They can't go wasting resources on every boat that comes through these waters."

"How do we get on, though?" Jesse asked. "They raised the ramp. It operates from up top, not down below."

Zebedee had already been considering this. "If we can get up to it," he said, "if *one* of us can get up to it, it's an easy climb from there onto the ship."

"Not even *you* can jump that high," said Jesse.

"We figure it's up around five or six metres," said Zebedee.

"But we think we know a way," added Annie.

"It's going to take someone light and strong," Zebedee said, looking straight at me.

"And somebody *big* and strong," Annie said, smiling at Nish.

Nish looked like he was about to have a heart attack.

If someone had warned me earlier about what was to happen, I think I would have begged off the snowmobile ride out to see the ship.

I thought we were going to *look* at the ship – not *invade* it. And I thought there were *eight* of us – not just little ol' me being hung out to dry. Hung out, literally, it turned out.

"Here's the plan," Zebedee said, making eye contact with his mom to make sure they were in agreement, which they clearly were. "We use the ropes to get up there. I can throw a long rope so it lands on the ramp and drapes over the far side. If we can pull it down so we have both ends at ground level, we can use the rope to haul Travis up."

I tried to swallow, but it felt like firecrackers were going off in my chest.

"Travis is the lightest," Zebedee continued. "But we're going to need all the pulling-power we can get to haul him up there. The simple thing would be to use one of the snowmobiles, but we can't risk making all that noise."

We? I felt like screaming. Where's the *we* in Travis being thrown aboard a ship filled with pirates?

"That's where you come in, Nish," Zebedee said,

turning to the biggest, reddest face in the group.

"I'm not going up!" Nish practically sobbed. "I'm scared of heights, remember?"

"How could we forget?" said Sarah.

"We don't want you up," Zebedee said. "We need you down. You're our snowmobile."

Nish looked puzzled. He had no idea what Zebedee and his mom had planned.

We gathered up the ropes and sneaked back through the ice chessboard to the side of the ship. So far so good – not a sound, and nothing from the ship.

Zebedee and his mom began working a long rope out of a bag. Annie tied a full water bottle to one end and Zebedee very carefully laid down the rope in a large coil, making sure none of the loops were twisted. He was being incredibly methodical. Perhaps that's what life in the North teaches you: do it right the first time, as there may not be a second chance!

I waited, watching, half hoping they wouldn't be able to get the rope over the ramp.

Zebedee threw, and the water bottle flew high, pulling the rope behind it as the coils unwound on the ice.

A complete miss. The rope looped high over the front of the ramp and the water bottle chunked back to the ground, the rope falling all around it in jumbles.

Zebedee carefully coiled the rope up again and threw a second time. This time the bottle clanged onto the ramp and bounced back off the wrong side and down.

We all moved in tight to the hull of the ship. If someone had heard the bottle hit, they might come and look. But if they just looked out, they wouldn't be able to see us under the curve of the hull.

We waited a few minutes — no sound from above — and then Zebedee and his mom moved out again to reset the rope and try once more. Annie this time picked up some of the coiled rope to gain a little height for Zebedee's toss.

Up, up, up sailed the water bottle, yanking the snaking rope behind. Up, up, and . . . over! The bottle pulled the rope down over the far side of the ramp and the rope went taut.

But the bottle had not come down far enough! It hung there in the air, just out of reach. And the rope itself seemed caught on the ramp. Annie tried feeding more rope out in the hope that the weight of the bottle would drag it farther down, but it didn't budge. She tried flicking the rope in the hope that it would loosen and drop. She tried pulling it back to free it. But nothing worked. The bottle remained just out of reach.

Sam and Sarah were already trying to lift each other up to it, but in their bulky snowmobile suits and heavy boots they were slipping and sliding.

"Leave it!" Zebedee commanded. "I'll get it."

We all went silent as Zebedee began taking off his big boots and snowmobile suit. When he was down to his track suit, he removed his socks. Here we were in the middle of the Arctic Ocean and he's in his *bare feet!* I looked around. No one was saying a word. No one was rolling their eyes or anything like that. It was almost as if this was what they'd expect of Zebedee.

He went off to the side then, crouched down on one knee, and rested his head on his other knee. He seemed almost in prayer, gathering himself for what he was about to try. Then he came back, took one look at Annie, who smiled, and did his quick two step hop. He shot up off one leg, into the air like he was rising off a trampoline. He leapt and reached and, amazingly, wrapped both hands around the water bottle.

He seemed to hang there a moment, and then we heard a quick scraping sound as the rope pulled free, and down came Zebedee.

He quickly scrambled back into his snowmobile suit and boots while Annie got to work on me. She had two harnesses out and was buckling them together and then tying the contraption around my chest.

"You're the lead dog now," she giggled.

"What?" I asked, confused as well as scared to death.

"These are dog harnesses," Zebedee explained. "For my mom's sled."

In a moment I was all harnessed up. Zebedee had untied the water bottle from the rope and was now working the end through steel rings on the harness.

It seemed insane, but Travis Lindsay, captain of the Screech Owls, was willing to do whatever it takes.

"Easy now!"

Zebedee was completely in charge of this mad scheme, but I was now its main element. I knew what I had to do. Get aboard, take some pictures – incriminating, if possible – and get off as fast I could. If we got the photos, we could use them as evidence and get the Mounties to send out an investigative unit.

Annie had hooked Nish and Zebedee up to harnesses as well. The two of them were at the other end of the rope and leaning in the opposite direction, digging in as best they could on the ice.

I felt the rope tighten, then start to lift me.

"Easy! Easy!" said Zebedee.

Nish grunted.

Up, up, up I rose. I wondered if this was what angels felt like as they went up to heaven. I looked down, and watched the faces of Rachel, Sam, Sarah, Jesse, and Annie grow smaller and smaller. I could see Zebedee and Nish – Nish ploughing steadily ahead like a workhorse.

I looked up. The ramp was within reach. Now I

had to figure out how to get onto the ramp from below it.

I grabbed the ramp with one hand and swung my body back and forth, back and forth, until it seemed I might swing right off. I put all my weight into the last swing and hooked my left leg up onto the ramp, my knee tightening against the steel as if I'd turned into a human clamp.

Now I worked my other hand higher on the rope until I could swing my right leg onto the ramp too. Finally, I rolled over onto my back, flat now on the ramp.

I'd made it! Not a sound from below, but I knew they were cheering inside.

I got onto my knees and unbuckled the harness. The ramp was a little shaky as it was suspended almost straight out from the deck.

I kept in a crouch, trying to move quickly but as carefully as possible. I couldn't make any noise. And I couldn't afford a slip – not at this height!

I made it to the rail of the ship and stepped over, landing lightly on the deck.

So far, so good.

Zebedee had had me tuck Data's camera into my jacket pocket, so I took it out now and turned it on.

I took several photographs of this side of the deck. There was really nothing special that I could make out. Two lifeboats under tarps, some ventilation ducts, several communication and satellite devices standing high over the pilot cabin.

And then I heard something.

A crash – something hitting metal, hard.

A *roar* – long, deep, steady, then fading.

The engine! They must be firing up the engine!

But the ship was anchored. The helicopter was gone. The hunting party was still out there somewhere. The engine was probably just being fired up for a test. Or to generate electricity. Or maybe for heat.

I pressed myself against a steel wall and waited for the sound of anyone moving about. But there was nothing. No voices. No steps. Nothing.

The helicopter pad! I must get shots of the landing pad!

I moved along the deck, staying as low as possible, and headed for the stern of the ship, where the landing pad rose up high. I had to climb up to the aft deck, much smaller, in order to shoot some pictures, but it was the only way to show the bull's-eye target for landing and all the safety lights.

Still, what was illegal about a helicopter landing pad? And what was illegal about heading off in a hunting party – especially if they had proper licences?

I realized I still had nothing.

But then I heard another crash, followed by a roar.

And another crash. And another.

And a roar.

That was no engine!

The sound was coming from the far side of the ship. If I was to find out what was making it, I would have to go back down from the aft deck and make my away around the stern, under the helicopter pad, to the far side. There was no other choice.

Carefully, I went back down the metal steps, going backwards for safety. I couldn't make a sound. If I fell, the clatter would bring someone out for sure.

I got to the main deck and began making my way around the stern. I wished my snowmobile suit was white, for camouflage, not blue. But too late now for such considerations.

I came to the final turn, and froze.

Voices!

No, a *single* voice. And an angry one.

I didn't recognize the language, though I was convinced that this was cursing – no matter what language it was. Someone was swearing up a storm at something. But it was only a single voice, with no one answering back.

I peeked around and saw the boots of a man as he leaned over a barrier and tossed something. It looked . . . blubbery. Almost like that raw seal we'd been served at the banquet.

The man cursed again and turned, wiping his hand on his coveralls. He shivered from the wind and quickly stepped back inside. He was cold. Maybe he wouldn't come out again. Maybe I could see what it was he was swearing at.

Crouching so low I felt like a slug moving along the wall, I very slowly made my way along the deck, past the door he had just slammed shut. I could hear more banging. And some dull roaring sounds. And another sound, too. *The sound of flesh tearing.*

I got the camera ready. My hand was shaking badly. I held it with both hands to steady it, then swivelled quickly off the wall and stood up at the barrier.

I could not believe my eyes. In a cargo hold below me, a large polar bear in a cage was ripping apart the blubber the angry man had tossed down. The banging was coming from other cages, each with a polar bear in it with barely enough space to turn around.

I raised the camera and began snapping shots. There were six cages, five of them with bears inside. Each bear was being kept separate from the others, and from the growling and banging it seemed they would tear each other apart if the locks came undone.

I switched Data's camera over to video and did a long scan of the scene.

I felt sick to my stomach. The bears were almost howling. Some had blood on their coats. A couple were methodically bashing themselves into their cages, and one large bear had rubbed its fur down to a huge and horrible red welt on the side. How long had it been in that cage? I wondered.

I scanned back again, then turned the camera off and put it in my jacket pocket. The motion must have caught the attention of the bear that had been eating, because suddenly he angrily charged the bars of his cage.

With an enormous crash, he hit the front full on. It had the force of a car accident. The cage almost broke apart. I backed away quickly, ducking past the door just as I heard the handle begin to turn.

They say hockey is a game of inches – well, in that case spying must be a game of millimetres. I had barely passed the door when it opened.

The man stepped out, but instead of facing me, he walked toward the barrier overlooking the caged bears. He was cursing again – you just knew he was using words that, if they were translated into English, would burn your ears off. He stomped hard on the deck and yelled at the bears while I crept back along the wall and slipped around the corner.

Success!

I moved quickly along the deck to the ramp on the other side, and was just stepping out onto the ramp when the shout came.

"*HEY!*"

I froze. I looked back, quickly. The man was hurrying down from the upper deck.

"Stop right there!" English now – though I took no comfort in that.

I reached for the rope, but there would never be enough time.

Zebedee was already out, waving his arms from below. "Jump!" he shouted. "Jump! Jump!"

His mother had a tarp out and was getting the others to grab corners – an orange sheet of heavy plastic and five people with their hands on it.

"*You little – !*" the man screamed. He was on the main deck now, his feet slipping as he scrambled down toward me.

I looked down.

I looked back.

I looked down again.

And I dropped . . .

16

Zebedee Okalik

SAM AND SARAH SAY I HAVE TO DO THIS ENTRY for their polar bear project. They say I'm part of the project now, so I have to contribute. I'll do my best.

They want me to tell the story about our escape from the ship. So here goes.

It was my mom's idea that we catch Travis in the tarp. She used to get us to play that game with a blanket when we were little. But in the children's game you do it out on the soft snow so if someone falls out they won't get hurt. You don't do it from the height of a two-storey building.

But it worked. We caught Travis fine. He rolled out of the tarp and onto the ground and we all scrambled away, my waste-conscious mom making sure to gather up the tarp as we went.

We started running toward the ice piles, where we had hidden the snowmobiles, and we were almost there when the first shot was fired.

I never heard a scream like that in all my life. I thought it was Sam or one of the other girls. But then I realized the screamer was right beside me. Nish.

Well, I can't blame him. I don't think he saw the ice exploding just to the side of him when that bullet whizzed into it, and I don't think I'll ever tell him how close he came to buying it.

We reached cover just as a second rifle shot pounded into a wall of ice close to Jesse.

"Get the rifles out!" Nish yelled at me.

"What for?" I asked.

"So we can fire back!"

I almost started to giggle. Did Nish think he was in some old Western on TV where we were about to have a shootout?

"He's going to be coming for us!" Nish said.

"Calm down," I said. "Even if he gets the ramp down by himself he has no snowmobile. They drove off on them – remember?"

Nish blushed red. "Oh yeah – I forgot."

"Let's get loaded up and be out of here," I said.

Travis, who hadn't spoken a word, started telling us what he had seen. We couldn't believe it. Sam started bawling.

What were they going to do with the bears? I kept wondering. Sell them to zoos?

It didn't matter what they were planning. There was no doubt it was illegal. Travis said he counted five bears – I sure hope he got some good photographs – and if so, that would be more polar bears than our entire village would see in a year.

And why did they kill the cubs? If they were for zoos, wouldn't it make more sense to take the cubs?

I was thinking all this on the ride back. We moved out quickly, keeping the blocks of ice between us and the ship. Once we hit more open ice, I revved up my machine and shot ahead.

The rest also started moving faster as well. We spread out, making good time.

And good thing, too.

If I hadn't been wearing my snowmobile helmet, I might have heard it coming.

But it wasn't the *whup-whup-whup* of the helicopter rotor I heard first: it was another sound, far more alarming.

Cccrrrrrrrack!
Cccrrrrrrrack!
Cccrrrrrrrack!

Someone was firing at us!

I saw ice chips fly up ahead of us on the right, then on the left. Then to the side. I looked back. The big helicopter from the ship was above us. I could see the side door open and a man with a rifle, aiming and firing.

Cccrrrrrrrack!

Cccrrrrrrrack!

Again, ice exploding in front of us.

My heart was pounding through my mouth. I can only imagine how terrified the others were.

I started to slow, the others following. But then it struck me. He wasn't trying to hit us – he couldn't possibly be that bad a shot – he was trying to get us to stop.

Sure enough, the helicopter got in front of us and began coming down. I knew then what they were up to. They were trying to find out what, if anything, we knew. And if we had any evidence – like, say, some incriminating photographs – they were going to take it and destroy it.

I gambled. Some might say a foolish gamble, but I took it anyway.

"*Move out again!*" I shouted to the snowmobilers.

"*But they'll kill us!*" someone screamed back. I didn't have to check to know who.

"*They won't do anything!*" I shouted. "*Go hard for Pang!*"

Mom was first to gun her machine and take off again. The girls followed, then the rest of us.

The helicopter rose again and followed, but not for long.

The moment Pang came into sight – far off still, but visible – they turned and hightailed it out of there.

What would they do? I wondered. Set sail as soon as they got back to the ship? Release the bears and hope we had no pictures?

I had no idea.

I was just glad we were back in Pang – and everyone was still alive.

Jenny Staples

I WAS FIRST TO SEE THEM COMING.

I had no idea snowmobiles could move so fast. I looked way out onto the ice and saw these little dark specks moving along and then realized what they were.

We knew from Zebedee's uncle that the kids had headed out. He said they were with Zebedee and Annie, who is a hunter, so there was nothing to worry about, they'd be fine.

But we *were* worried. Especially when lunchtime passed and then it was almost dinner and there was still no word from them and no one really knew where they were.

Mr. D. was in a dither. Even Muck, who never seems to worry about anything, had been seen checking his watch and standing down by the old whaling shed, staring out over the ice.

"It's them!" I shouted. "They're coming in!"

People came running down to the shore. It seemed like the entire village had been watching for them. I was one of the first down there, and when I looked back up it seemed people were swarming down by the hundreds – even though there aren't really that many people in all of Pang. I could see Mr. D. and Muck coming along, too, Muck carefully making his way down the gravel slope with his one bad leg.

Zebedee was first in, bringing his snowmobile rather dramatically to a sliding stop. He had Sam on behind. Then came Jesse with Sarah, Rachel with Travis, and Zebedee's mom with Nish hanging on behind.

Nish looked green. He looked like a combination of seasick, airsick, carsick, and snowmobile-sick. He got off in a daze, walked over back of the sheds where they keep the boats, and I could hear him starting to retch.

No one even bothered going to check him out. There was too much excitement. Sam was talking so fast it's a wonder her tongue didn't end up in a knot. It was almost impossible to make out what she was trying to tell us through her tears – something about polar bears and being shot at.

Sarah was a little better, but even she was exploding with words that were trying to get out before her brain could put them together.

They were talking about cages and rifle shots and being chased by a helicopter – it was absolutely wild. And it made no sense to any of us.

I felt a strong hand on my shoulder and looked up to see one of the Mounties, the older man, push through. The other Mountie, the young, good-looking one, was right behind him. When they came into the large circle that had formed around the returnees, everyone went quiet.

The older Mountie looked at Zebedee. "What's going on here, Zeb?"

Zebedee swallowed hard before speaking. It was the most amazing thing. A moment ago there had been screaming and crying, but now everyone went completely silent. (Well, not exactly everyone – now you could hear Nish again, hurling in the background.)

When Zebedee spoke, it was in his very quiet way, but he was so sure and careful with his words it sounded almost like he was making a speech. I was most impressed.

"We checked out the mystery ship," he told the Mountie, but was really telling everyone. "And we think they're involved in a polar bear smuggling operation."

The Mountie nodded, but was not convinced. "You'd need more proof than a dead cub or two, young man."

Zebedee turned to Travis.

"Trav," he said, "can you bring that camera here?"

Travis stepped forward, carefully pulling Data's camera out of his snowmobile jacket.

"Travis is the hero here," said Zebedee, smiling at Travis. "He's the one who went on board and got the pictures."

Travis, red-faced, handed the camera to the Mountie. The Mountie looked at the screen on the back and Travis came around to his side and talked him through the photos.

"And I got some of it on video, too," Travis said, changing the setting to show the Mountie.

"It's okay," the Mountie said. "I've seen all I need to."

The older Mountie turned to the younger one.

"Radio Iqaluit," he said. "Tell them we'll need everything we can get – including the Coast Guard."

Derek Dillinger

I MISS OUT ON EVERYTHING, IT SEEMS. WILSON and Willie and Gordie were heading off to golf and said they needed a fourth, so I tagged along and lost every single ball I hit.

I also lost out on all the excitement.

Maybe if I'd stuck with Jesse I'd have been in on the adventure, too.

Imagine that? Getting shot at! Getting chased by a helicopter! Getting to be heroes!

I think the last person I'd have expected to become a Hero of the North Pole was Travis Lindsay. He's such a little guy. But the way they tell the story, if Travis hadn't been small they could never have pulled it off.

Nishikawa, of course, is railing on about how he was the real hero, the "muscle" that got Travis up onto the ship in the first place, and how he was the guy who caught Travis when he had to jump.

Nish also claims it was his yelling – more likely screaming – that alerted the others to the helicopter attack.

Let him say what he wants. Fahd used his cellphone camera to get some photographic evidence of his own: Nish back of the boat shed when everyone else was gathered around the Mounties. Nish on his knees, throwing up. Some hero!

And for some reason, he hadn't been yelling "I'M GONNA HURL!" beforehand like it was the funniest thing anyone ever said.

It didn't take long for the RCMP and the Coast Guard to swing into action. Both Mounties from Pang set out on snowmobiles to set up a watch on the ship. And within a couple of hours there was a Defence chopper coming in from the military base in Alert.

The ship weighed anchor and took off, but the Coast Guard moved in on them before they could reach international waters. The five polar bears were still aboard, and all the men involved in the operation were arrested and charged with so many different offences – including attempted murder – that I couldn't possible keep them straight.

But none of this answered the question of *why*. Why had they killed the cubs? Why had they taken adult bears and caged them? Why had they been so desperate to keep their operation a secret that they'd been willing to fire at a bunch of kids on snowmobiles?

It made no sense at all. At least not until the next day.

19

Jeremy Weathers

I'M TO REPORT ON THE PRESS CONFERENCE
that is about to start in the community centre.

Nish is walking around like he's a Hollywood
celebrity, which is really rather pathetic when
you consider what a tiny role he played in this
whole story.

Zebedee and Travis, on the other hand, are the
real heroes, though you'd never know it. Both of
them are so quiet and humble it's almost as if they're
delighted to let Nish steal their thunder.

A commissioner from the RCMP is here, as well as
several other officers. There's a general from the
Armed Forces. And about a dozen dark-suited civil
servants from Ottawa who are running around like
they are the busiest and most important people on
the face of the earth.

The RCMP commissioner is speaking:

"Thank you all for coming here to Pangnirtung this morning. We appreciate your coming on such short notice.

"The Royal Canadian Mounted Police has laid a total of 246 charges this morning in Superior Court in Iqaluit. The charges range from attempted murder to a series of charges concerning the capture and transport of an endangered species. A full list of the charges, as well as details on those individuals charged, will be handed out in a moment.

"First, however, the Government of Canada would like to express its appreciation to the people of Pangnirtung. Special commendation is made for Mrs. Annie Okalik and her son, Zebedee Okalik. And we would also like to offer our deepest appreciation to the following young men and women from the towns of Tamarack and Waskaganish:

"Travis Lindsay [who blushed and stared at his shoes]

"Samantha Bennett [who dabbed her eyes]

"Sarah Cuthbertson [who smiled]

"Jesse Highboy [who pretended they were speaking about someone else]

"Rachel Highboy [who smiled at Travis]

"And Wayne Nishikawa [who pumped a fist in the air like he'd just scored a winning goal]

"Without the assistance, the sharp-witted decisions

and, yes, the bravery of these young people, these charges might never have been laid.

"The RCMP believes that this ship, the *Northern Star* – registered in St. Lucia – was involved in a highly detailed and organized scheme to capture a number of mature polar bears and sequester those bears on a small disputed island that lies between the Canadian Arctic claims and the territorial waters of Greenland.

"The charges will allege that the plan had been to build a reserve of mature bears with the idea that they would mate and create a continual supply of polar bears in this disputed no man's land, and that a fly-in operation would then be created with the idea of bringing big-game hunters to the island to hunt the bears.

"Given that polar bears are now considered an endangered species, given that the United States has seen fit to ban the importation of polar bear fur or trophies of any kind, and given, as well, that sport hunting of the bears has almost completely vanished around the world, we believe the plan was to charge a premium price – perhaps as much as one million dollars – to unethical but very wealthy big-game hunters from around the world.

"Had the *Northern Star* reached its destination with the captured bears, there may well have been nothing we could have done, given that this disputed island is, at least for the time being, out of our jurisdiction.

"Had these brave young men and women not been able to discover what was happening – and further to produce photographic evidence that will be critical to any future criminal proceedings – the polar bear population surrounding Pangnirtung would have been decimated. And not only would the bears have suffered, obviously, but the people of Pangnirtung, many of whom still live the traditional Inuit life, would have suffered as well.

"The RCMP is pleased to report, then, that all five captured polar bears have since been treated and released, including one female who has since been reunited with her two cubs, both of which would have perished within days had this action not been taken."

At which point, predictably, Sam burst into tears.

Wilson Kelly

I'D LIKE TO KEEP THIS SHORT, AS I AM NOT much for writing. But Mr. D. says I have to contribute and I've been assigned to bring everyone up to date on what took place after the RCMP press conference.

It seemed the reporters and all the uniformed officials were gone as fast as they'd arrived and Pang was quiet again.

And that's when we remembered: we had a hockey tournament to finish!

Muck and Mr. D. had us all gather together in a room in the little hotel. Mr. D. mentioned again the honour that had just been paid to the Screech Owls, but he was careful to say he didn't approve of kids skipping out like that on their own.

"You could have been killed," he kept saying.

And every time he said it, Nish would say, "I know, I know" – as if he had been the only one in any danger.

Muck simply said "good work" to the kids who had found out about the ship, and then he shifted back to being the Screech Owls' coach.

"The tournament kind of got lost," he said. "That's fine by me. This trip has been far more about learning things – a *lot* of things – than it ever was about hockey.

"But we have one more game to play. One more. The Iqaluit Ice Dogs, probably the best team in the tournament, had a couple of off games and they're out. The Resolute Rebels never stood a chance.

"So that leaves us and the host team, the Polar Bears, to play in the final. The Governor General will be in attendance. I want you to think about that, but I also want you to think about what you've seen here and learned here. You need to respect the Polar Bears, who aren't all that strong a team, with one obvious exception."

"Zebedee," Fahd whispered, completely unnecessarily.

"And so," Muck continued, "I want to see clean, fair, and respectful play. You do hear me, don't you, Nishikawa?"

Nish looked up, eyes blinking like an innocent choirboy.

"Yes, sir, coach."

Willie Granger

HARD TO BELIEVE THAT WE'RE GOING HOME in the morning. This has been the greatest experience of my life. And in some ways the strangest. I can't believe I've never left Canada. We've played in Sweden and Japan and Australia and Florida – but this place is more different than any of them, except perhaps Japan. But it's still *Canada*. Go figure.

The kids are all pumped for the final match, Screech Owls against Polar Bears. We tied 3–3 in the first meeting, and ever since we've been talking about what it would be like to play them again. Nish has probably devised a dozen different strategies for containing Zebedee.

From what I saw of Zebedee Okalik's play in that first game, Nish might like to put him in one of those polar bear cages and throw away the key.

We came over early to get ready. The jerseys were all freshly washed and smelled almost like perfume, causing all sorts of insults and stupid cracks from Nish – and about Nish. But I kind of liked the smell.

I was going to say something about it to Travis, when he suddenly pulled his jersey on over his head and I would swear – absolutely swear – I heard and sort-of saw Travis kiss the inside as the crest and "C" for captain slipped past his face.

Well, each to his own, I say. Weird or what?

Mr. D. had the portable skate sharpener up and running, and the grinding metal and the trail of sparks made another smell. One of my very favourites. Dmitri was trying to put a slightly larger curve on his stick by working it under a door and prying it up. Sam was lost in thought. Sarah was smiling and chatting away happily as she laced up her skates. Nish had his head down between his knees. At least this time he wasn't barfing.

All things I've seen before. But when Nish goes into this mode – head down, barely breathing, face out of sight – you know he expects to have a big game. We laugh at him, but you have to admit that when the game gets tough, no one plays harder than the puffed-up, insufferable Nishikawa.

Muck came in just before we were to go on the ice.

He walked to the centre of the dressing room, looked around, said nothing, and walked out.

Quite a speech for Muck, I'd say.

Andy Higgins

MUCK STARTED MY LINE!

I couldn't believe it. Any important game in the past and it's always been Sarah's line, with Dmitri on right wing and Travis on left. But this time it was me and Derek with little Simon on my right. What an honour!

I had to take the faceoff against Zebedee Okalik, which was pretty intimidating after what he did to us first game. I'd watched him in the warm-up, and he was acting like this was nothing more than a game of road hockey in the driveway, with no one even keeping score – not a championship game with the Governor General of Canada there to hand out the medals.

How can someone be so happy-go-lucky? I was so jumpy before the game, I could hardly tie my laces. I thought I was going to throw up. Okay, don't worry, I didn't – I'm *not* Nish.

I went into the faceoff circle the way I like to: head down, stick across my knees while I twirl the blade a couple of times.

Zebedee comes into the faceoff like he's come for dinner or something. "How ya doing?" he says with that big gap-toothed smile.

"Fine!" I grunted, and instantly felt stupid.

I'm used to trash talk – guys calling me names and laughing at my height and things like that. None of that ever bothers me. But this guy comes across so friendly, I almost took off my glove and reached out to shake his hand after I got over the shock.

"Ready, boys?" the ref says, raising both hands to check the goal lights at each end.

We nodded – and the game was on.

I won the draw. I tried Sarah's trick of plucking the puck out of mid-air as it fell, and for once it worked. I sent the puck back to Sam, waiting on defence. Sam clipped it back off the boards to little Simon, and he tried to hit me with a blind pass off the backhand.

Dumb idea.

Zebedee picked the puck up – it was almost as if he had been reading Simon's notes for the big game – and tore down the ice so fast I barely had time to turn back before he was cutting around Wilson on the far defence and then using his body to force his way in front of the net.

A quick deke, and Zebedee had Jeremy down and out, allowing him to flick the puck high into our net.

Probably the last time Muck ever starts my line.

Sarah Cuthbertson

I HAD A SICKENING FEELING WHEN I SAW SIMON try and guess where Andy would be. He guessed right – but only if Zebedee hadn't been on the ice!

No wonder Muck gets so disgusted with blind passes.

Down 1–0 on the first shift of the game is a situation no one likes to find themselves in. We'd have to find a way to work our way back.

It didn't happen for a while. Jeremy got lucky when a Polar Bear shot went off the post, and big Gordie Griffiths shot too high on a chance for us. But I could feel it coming. We were getting stronger every shift.

Just before the end of the first period, I picked up a loose puck in our end and put it off the boards to Nish, who'd moved in behind our net. He put it off the boards to me again, and I instantly put it back the same way to him.

Some of the people in the stands booed. It may have looked like we were unsure what to do, but we knew exactly what we were doing. Nish was waiting for Dmitri to break. The moment he saw Dmitri skate hard out of our own end, Nish sent his big high "football" pass down the ice.

Once again, it worked perfectly. The puck floated high over the blue line and Dmitri knocked it down on the first bounce, already on a breakaway. The play was just too fast and Dmitri too quick for the slower Polar Bears – with one exception, of course. But Zebedee wasn't on the ice.

Dmitri came in fast and faked a forehand to go to his backhand. But this time the goalie was ready. He'd seen that play before and guessed right, sticking hard to Dmitri as Dmitri headed for the corner.

Sometimes I wonder at how incredibly fast Dmitri's brain works. He saw in an instant what the goalie was doing, held his shot, and slipped the puck backwards through his own skates.

Travis was coming in hard, looking for a rebound, and suddenly found himself all alone in front of an empty net with a pass coming perfectly onto his blade.

Polar Bears 1, Screech Owls 1.

We have a game!

24

Travis Lindsay

I HAVEN'T SCORED A BIG GOAL IN A LONG TIME —
and did it ever feel great!

We were tied after one period, and tied again
after the second, when Sam scored on a screen shot
from the point and Zebedee Okalik scored his
second of the game on an amazing play. Zebedee
tucked the puck back into his skates and swept
around Fahd so fast, Fahd was still looking for what
he thought was a drop pass when Zebedee scored
through Jeremy's five-hole.

Muck came in and talked to us between the
second and the third — most unusual for him.

"Good game," he said, and then walked out.

"Sure is a yapper!" Nish cracked when Muck was
out of earshot.

Nish was playing hard. His face looked like he'd
boiled it, and sweat was absolutely flying everywhere.
The smell coming off his disgusting equipment bag

and his soaked uniform was almost enough to make me gag. So much for the freshly washed jerseys.

But it was also a good smell. It meant Nish was fully into the game. And any game that gets the full 100 percent Nishikawa is a game worth watching.

The third period was going to be great.

We headed out after a fresh flood with the arena packed. I checked where the Governor General was sitting, and not a person had moved. The entire rink seemed to be holding its breath.

Zebedee made his move early in the third, picking up a puck at centre and coming in hard on Nish and Fahd. He tried to slip the puck between them again and leap through, but the boys cut him off perfectly. It looked like accidental contact and the referee never even raised his whistle. Not hard to tell he had never seen Nish before!

A while later, with our line on, Dmitri grabbed a loose puck in the neutral zone and snaked in along the boards in the Polar Bear end. He paused, stick-handling nicely, and Zebedee went for him, trying to force him to make a play. Dmitri did, but not one Zebedee expected. He simply left the puck where it was and stepped back.

The move caught Zebedee entirely by surprise. He flew right past the puck, and when he tried to turn to grab it, he smashed shoulder-first into the boards, losing his stick, which rattled into the corner.

Dmitri could have hit Sarah back of the Polar Bear net but chose instead to send a long saucer pass to Nish, stepping in from the blue line.

Zebedee tried to stop Nish with his skates, but Nish knew he had no stick and, instead of passing to me, tried his new spinnerama move. It worked, and he was instantly in tight on the Polar Bear goal.

A defenceman dove to stop Nish's shot.

The shot clipped off the defender's stick and looped high in the air – almost as if Nish were tossing horseshoes instead of shooting on net.

Up, up, up the puck spun, then down, down, down. It was like watching the slowest-motion replay in hockey history.

I had a perfect angle on it. I could tell, all the way, that the puck was going to loop high over everyone's head, even the reaching goaltender, and fall perfectly into the net.

Nish was going to be the hero!

But then – *snick!*

I have never in my life seen anything like it – never even imagined anything like it was possible.

If the puck looked like it was spinning in slow motion, Zebedee Okalik looked like he was *flying* in slow motion.

I don't know how he did it, but I saw him rise like a bird over the fallen defenceman, over Nish's shoulders, Nish's arms already raising his stick to celebrate, over the outstretched glove hand of the Polar Bears little goalie — and *snick!*

One quick little kick of the skate and the puck was "punted" to safety by Zebedee, flying harmlessly into the corner.

I saw the referee raise his whistle to his mouth, then pull it out and look dumbstruck. What had he just seen? What rule would apply?

None. No goal. No penalty. No whistle.

One of the Polar Bear defenders sliced the puck down the ice for icing and finally we had a stoppage in play.

Nish just skated around with his head down low, shaking it every now and then as if he might be dreaming.

We all skated back for the faceoff and I saw Zebedee skate past Nish and whack him on his big bottom.

I could hear Zebedee singing again: "*Wonderful feeling, feeling this way!*"

But this time it was different. This time, Nish was laughing.

Wayne Nishikawa

NISH'S FINAL JOURNAL ENTRY:
NOT TO BE RELEASED TO THE PUBLIC IN THE LIFE-
TIME OF WAYNE NISHIKAWA!

The Ol' Nisherama here one more time for all you fans.

Okay, I admit it. I have never in my life seen a play like that. I have to give Zippy credit. I was already getting into my celebration when he somehow jumped halfway to the rafters and kicked that puck to safety.

I don't care that he was singing. I thought it was funny. I even like the crazy kid now.

After all, if it hadn't been for Zippy 'n' me – those polar bears would never have been saved.

It was me 'n' Zip who got Travis up there, me 'n' Zip who caught him, me who warned about the helicopter, and Zip who led the charge home.

All Travis did was push a stupid button on Data's camera.

There were only a couple of minutes left after Zippy robbed me of the goal that would have, once again, won a major tournament for the Screech Owls.

Muck had me on in the final minute, of course, and Sarah had one great chance when I sent her in on a breakaway – sadly, she doesn't have my hands and put it off the crossbar.

That puck bounced out to the blue line. Normally, I would have anticipated it perfectly – I have the best hockey sense, by far, of any of the Owls, you know – but I could see Zippy just standing there, like a racehorse, waiting for the bar to lift so he could bolt.

He grabbed the puck and took off. I was already back, skating effortlessly in reverse.

I knew my options. I could ride him off into the corner. I could poke check him. I could, if need be, take him out with a hip check that would throw him into next week.

He came down fast and – can you believe this! – tried my own patented spinnerama move.

And I let him go.

I could have had him easily, but I knew how much it meant to him to be a hero in front of the hometown crowd – especially with the Governor General in the building.

That's the way I am, you know. I had the game won, as usual, when he got lucky. And I could have had him, easily, if I'd really wanted to.

Instead, I let him go.

Zippy took Jeremy out easily and rang one in off the bar. Not a bad shot.

Polar Bears 4, Owls 3.

They got the medals. We got little carved inuk-shuks.

I feel good about that.

Some of the Owls think I only care about myself.

This is proof that they're wrong.

Muck Munro

MUCK HERE.

I do have one point to make.

Just in case anyone ever wonders, Nishikawa got faked out of his jockstrap on the winning goal.

That's all.

THE END

THE SCREECH OWLS SERIES

Also available in five omnibus editions!

Newmarket Public Library

Ron Devries

Roy MacGregor has been involved in hockey all his life. Growing up in Huntsville, Ontario, he competed for several years against a kid named Bobby Orr, who was playing in nearby Parry Sound. He later returned to the game when he and his family settled in Ottawa, where he worked for the *Ottawa Citizen* and became the Southam National Sports Columnist. He still plays old-timers hockey and was a minor-hockey coach for more than a decade.

Roy MacGregor is the author of several classics in the literature of hockey. *Home Game* (written with Ken Dryden) and *The Home Team* (nominated for the Governor General's Award for Non-fiction) were both No. 1 national bestsellers. He has also written the game's best-known novel, *The Last Season*. His most recent non-fiction hockey book is *A Loonie for Luck*, the true story of the famous good-luck charm that inspired Canada's men and women to win hockey gold at the Salt Lake City Winter Olympics. His other books include *A Life in the Bush*, *Escape*, *The Weekender*, *The Dog and I*, and *Canadians*.

Roy MacGregor is currently a columnist for the *Globe and Mail*. He lives in Kanata, Ontario, with his wife, Ellen. They have four children, Kerry, Christine, Jocelyn, and Gordon.

You can talk to Roy MacGregor at **www.screechowls.com**.